Micha...
a big...
been deadly.

Natalie couldn't think someone in this lab wanted her gone so badly they'd tampered with the brakes of her rental. Hunching forward, she planted her hands on the table. "I don't believe I've been marked for death, as you so elegantly put it. But what if someone just wanted to scare me off, send me back to DC with my tail between my legs?"

"Anyone who's talked to you for five minutes knows that's not going to work." He brushed some crumbs from the table into his hand and tipped them into the trash. "Is it going to scare you off?"

She tossed her hair back over her shoulder. "Of course not, but I'm going to be looking at people through a different set of eyes."

"That's a good policy, anyway." He stopped at the door and twisted his head over his shoulder. "I can check under your hood, if you like."

She raised her eyebrows. "That sounds like an improper proposal."

"I wish..."

CRIME LAB COLD CASE

CAROL ERICSON

Harlequin

INTRIGUE

Harlequin®
INTRIGUE™

Recycling programs for this product may not exist in your area.

ISBN-13: 978-1-335-08205-3

Crime Lab Cold Case

Copyright © 2025 by Carol Ericson

Harlequin Enterprises ULC
22 Adelaide St. West, 41st Floor
Toronto, Ontario M5H 4E3, Canada
www.Harlequin.com

Printed in U.S.A.

Carol Ericson is a bestselling, award-winning author of more than forty books. She has an eerie fascination for true-crime stories, a love of film noir and a weakness for reality TV, all of which fuel her imagination to create her own tales of murder, mayhem and mystery. To find out more about Carol and her current projects, please visit her website at www.carolericson.com, "where romance flirts with danger."

Books by Carol Ericson

Harlequin Intrigue

Pacific Northwest Forensics

The Creekside Murder
Crime Lab Cold Case

A Discovery Bay Novel

Misty Hollow Massacre
Point of Disappearance
Captured at the Cove
What Lies Below

The Lost Girls

Canyon Crime Scene
Lakeside Mystery
Dockside Danger
Malice at the Marina

Visit the Author Profile page at Harlequin.com.

CAST OF CHARACTERS

Michael Wilder—With his wife recently murdered, this forensics lab manager has more to worry about than the FBI's audit of cold cases, but the attractive special agent who shows up to do the audit offers him solace, both professionally and personally.

Natalie Brunetti—The FBI agent sent to conduct an audit of mishandlings at a forensics lab has ulterior motives, as her best friend went missing from this area fourteen years ago, and she needs an answer to the mystery—with or without the help of the tempting lab manager.

Katie Fellows—Natalie's best friend, who disappeared fourteen years ago, just might be the catalyst to solving the murder of Michael's wife.

Deputy Max Reynolds—This sheriff's deputy was quick to dismiss Katie as a runaway; was his inappropriate interest in her the reason why?

Jacob Reynolds—The deputy's son works in the forensics lab and has ample opportunity to make sure his father is protected.

Nicole Meloan—She controls the evidence receiving room at the lab with an iron fist, which may be why she's so anxious to befriend the FBI agent conducting the audit.

Dr. Phil Volosin—The head of the DNA lab has been around a long time—long enough to have altered evidence in several cold cases for his own purposes.

Chapter One

Natalie bolted upright, her heart pounding in her chest, her T-shirt soaked with sweat. Her wide eyes darted around the darkened bedroom, searching for an anchor, but the relentless green of the forest closed in on her. Her legs bicycled under the sheets, running from her dream, running from him.

Trapped in the tangled bedcovers, she thrust out her arms, clawing through the branches, scrabbling for an escape. Her hand hit a hard object, knocking it to the ground...the floor, where it shattered.

Her gaze shifted toward a glimmer of light that peeked through a crack in the blinds. Windows. A streetlight. Her bedroom.

Closing her eyes, she fell back against her pillow. The dream had come at her like a sledgehammer, annihilating the fragile facade she'd pieced together for the past fourteen years to cover her trauma.

Maybe it was about time she dismantled that facade and faced her fears.

LATER THAT MORNING, Natalie parked her suitcase in the lobby of the FBI office where she worked in Quantico. When Francesca, sitting at the front desk, stopped speaking into her headset, Natalie pointed at her bag. "Okay if I leave this here while I run upstairs and collect a few things?"

Francesca nodded. "You're traveling today?"

"Long flight to the West Coast." Natalie wrinkled her nose and patted the carry-on strapped across her body. "I just need to pick up some files before I leave."

"Go ahead. I'll…" Francesca answered a call and pointed at her eyes with two fingers, then aimed those fingers at Natalie's suitcase.

Natalie left her to it and hustled up the stairs to the records office. She dropped into a chair in front of one of the computers and logged in with her smart card. There was no way around leaving a trail. If anyone bothered to check, she could excuse her interest in these two missing-persons cold cases as being related to her assignment with the Marysville forensics lab. They *were* related.

She searched the database for the two cases and didn't even have to review them—she knew them by heart. She printed out both and grabbed two file folders from the supply cabinet.

The door to the office swung open with a bang, and she clutched the folders to her chest and spun around.

Special Agent Jefferson barreled into the room, and Natalie sidled in front of the printer, now spitting out pages of the first report. "Were you looking for me?"

Jefferson ran a hand over his bald head, as if he'd just broken into a sweat instead of her. "Agent Brunetti, didn't we give you a final briefing yesterday?"

Natalie swallowed and held up the folder before plucking a stack of papers from the printer and stuffing them inside. "Just dropped by to pick up a few more cases. I'm ready to go, sir. My flight leaves in a few hours."

Jefferson shook back the sleeve of his expensive navy suit and glanced at his even more expensive watch. "Better get going. Dulles is no picnic in the afternoon."

"I brought my bags to the office. I'm leaving for the airport straight from here." She slid the second set of papers into the other folder and crammed both folders into the bag at her feet. Then she yanked the bag up by the strap and hitched it over her shoulder.

"You're ambitious. I'll give you that, Brunetti." Stepping back, Jefferson narrowed his eyes. "Aren't you from that area? Seattle or something?"

She dipped her chin. "My family lived there for a while."

"It's good you have some familiarity with the location." He leveled a finger at her. "You're not going to be welcome there. You're an outsider, digging into their business, examining what they did wrong, telling them how to improve."

Natalie held up one hand in a stop sign. "I'll be diplomatic. We all want the same thing…to solve those cold cases."

"We do want to solve the cold cases, and the King County Sheriff's Department can get back to that business after we do ours—find out why and how so much evidence in that forensics lab in Marysville got corrupted or lost. The lab supervisor, Michael Wilder, should be happy to help. He wasn't in charge when the evidence got compromised. As far as we can tell, he's been running a tight ship."

"Has he, though?" Natalie tilted her head and readjusted the bag's strap on her shoulder. "The lab had evidence from the Kitsap Killer case just a few months ago and didn't run a basic test for a sex identifier, which would've solved that case earlier."

"That wasn't Wilder's call. The sample was sent to Seattle."

"His lab was responsible for the case."

Holding up a finger, Jefferson said, "Diplomacy, remember?"

"Got it. Now I'd better order my car for the airport, or I'm going to undiplomatically miss my flight." She made a move for the door, and Agent Jefferson shifted his stout frame out of her way.

She waved her hand in the air as she walked down the corridor, feeling his eyes boring into her back. She squared her shoulders and straightened her spine.

She had a feeling Jefferson had objected to sending her out to Seattle to look into the anomalies at the forensics lab in Marysville, but she did good work. Nobody could dispute that—even though she had some personality issues.

But she had a job to do and an ulterior motive for doing it, and she didn't really care what the lab rats in Marysville thought about her...especially Michael Wilder.

MICHAEL PUSHED HIS laptop away and massaged his throbbing temples. He'd been working all week to prep his lab's files for the FBI oversight inspection. He'd cleaned up a mess when he took over as manager for the forensics lab in

Marysville, but all his hard work over the past few years hadn't even scratched the surface of the mishandling of evidence that had occurred ten to fifteen years ago.

He smacked his hand on his desk, sending the pens and pencils in the holder into a frenzy. Rubbing the spot on the blotter he'd just hit, he lifted his head and peered at the cubicles outside his office window. Had anyone witnessed his flare of temper?

After the year he'd had, his bosses with the Washington State Patrol had mandated therapy for him. He hated talking to a shrink as much as he hated getting ready for some nosy FBI agent poking around his lab, but he had to admit the anger-management exercises Dr. Russell had been drilling into him seemed to be working. Until now.

As he dug his fists into his eyes, someone knocked on the open door. Michael blinked as he focused on Nicole Meloan's curly mop, as she stuck her head inside his office. Nicole ran Evidence Receiving, and she'd been putting in as many extra hours as he'd been. "Are you still here, Nicole?"

"I could ask you the same thing, but I have a feeling I know why we're both here after hours." Nicole pursed her lips, her usually pleasant face contorting into a frown.

She looked as mad as he felt, but he had to set an example. Michael took a deep breath through his nose and let it out slowly through his lips—another one of his coping mechanisms. "I appreciate your getting everything in order in the evidence room. It won't be so bad. A lot of what Agent Brunetti will be looking at is evidence compromised before our time. That'll keep him too busy to snoop around our current evidence and practices."

Nicole screwed up one side of her mouth. "I hope so. I have a process in my area."

"Don't we all." Michael twirled a finger in the air. "You should get out of here."

"On my way." She tucked a wild lock of hair behind one ear. "D-do you need anything? Are you alright? Is Ivy okay?"

Michael refrained from rolling his eyes. His staff meant well, but damn. Was it ever going to stop? His lips stretched into a smile. "I'm good, Nicole. My sister, Molly, is still here, and Ivy's thrilled. You go ahead. I'll see you bright and early tomorrow when we have our meeting with Agent Brunetti. Don't worry. We'll show him how we get things done around here."

"We sure will." She wiggled her fingers in the air as she turned.

Michael slumped in his chair. Did it look like he wasn't doing okay? He'd worked hard to get back to okay. Did everyone else just see right through him?

Closing his eyes, he massaged the back of his neck for one minute, then packed up his laptop and grabbed his jacket from the hook by the door. He'd already missed dinner and the bedtime rituals, so he might as well make it an even later night.

As he left the lab itself, he made sure the self-locking door closed behind him. The forensics lab had a lobby area with a security guard manning the front desk.

The soles of Michael's shoes plodded across the vinyl flooring that extended from the lab to the lobby, causing Miles to glance up. When he saw Michael, he saluted. "Working late again, chief?"

"Story of my life, Miles." Michael rapped on the desk as he walked by. "You got the good shift again, huh?"

Holding up a textbook, Miles said, "Nice and quiet for studying…but I never said that."

"My lips are sealed, but when you're done with school and I need a nurse, I'm counting on you for special treatment."

"You got it, man."

Michael pushed through the glass doors and inhaled the fresh, pine-scented air. He hadn't left the building all day, and the moist droplets that clung to his face and hair refreshed him. He wouldn't tell Dr. Russell he'd been cooped up all day. Getting plenty of fresh air came under the heading of anger management. Once this Nat Brunetti person did his thing at the lab and left, Michael planned on getting back to normal hours...until the next crisis.

The beep of his remote echoed in the nearly empty parking lot, despite the mist that seemed to mute every other sound. Before sliding behind the wheel of his truck, he placed his bag on the passenger seat.

He dropped onto the driver's seat and cranked the engine. He clutched the steering wheel as the truck idled. He didn't have to do this. These nighttime visits to the scene of the crime didn't help matters. That lonely stretch of trail didn't have any answers for him. The scant evidence the killer left behind had already been bagged and tagged a long time ago—and he hadn't been allowed to see any of it.

Grunting, he threw his truck into gear and stepped on the accelerator. He wanted to get this out of his system before the meeting with the FBI tomorrow. He needed the fresh air, anyway. Dr. Russell would approve...sort of.

Michael wheeled out of the parking lot of the lab and hit the road. The truck practically drove itself toward the forest of the national park. He drove past the turnoff for the camping area and continued into the heart of the woods.

If not aware of the trail head tucked behind some boxwood bushes, it could be missed, especially at night with no cars parked along the road. But he knew all about it.

Michael pulled his truck onto the soft shoulder as much as possible and cut the engine. He slid from the truck and eased the door closed. Flicking on his flashlight, he parted the bushes to reach the trailhead.

To this day, he couldn't figure out what Raine was doing on this trail. She'd never hiked a day in her life. He stepped carefully onto the moist ground, which was scattered with leaves, his work shoes no replacement for a pair of hiking boots.

His flashlight illuminated the trail in front of him, and he followed it to the first bend. A soft moan reached out to him across the still air, and he tripped to a stop as he saw a figure crouched in the darkness.

Adrenaline pumped through his body, and he lunged forward, one hand outstretched. "Raine!"

The person on the ground jumped to her feet, her face a white oval in the darkness, eyes glittering like a deer caught in the beam from his flashlight.

"Stop!" She thrust her arms in front of her, as if to ward him off. "I won't let you kill me like you killed her."

Chapter Two

Natalie squinted into the light, which was blinding her, her mouth dry, her fight-or-flight instinct on high alert. The large figure loomed in front of her, his arm extended as if to grab her.

He couldn't be the man from her past, but his presence in the woods at night, alone, signaled danger. She shoved one hand into a pocket, curling her fingers around the cold metal of her weapon.

Then she spun away like a startled fox, and crashed through the bushes back toward the campsite, where she'd left her car. The man yelled behind her, which made her propel her legs to pump harder through the underbrush, snapping twigs and crushing dry leaves beneath the soles of her sneakers.

If he tried to follow her, she'd shoot first and ask questions later. To hell with her career. She'd vowed never to be a victim again, and she'd kept that promise to herself...and to Katie. When she reached the edge of the empty campsite, she doubled over, wedging her hands on her knees. Her heavy breathing and pulse pounding in her ears blocked the noises from the forest.

When she caught her breath, she straightened up and tilted her head, her ears attuned to any sounds of footsteps or running. A few birds twittered, scolding her for upsetting their nighttime peace, and some animals rustled in the underbrush, but no human sounds reached her.

On shaky legs, she made it to her rental car in the campsite's parking area. She peeked into the back seat and checked her tires before dropping behind the wheel and drilling the ignition button with her knuckle to start the engine.

The stranger who'd accosted her back on the trail would hear her car if he was still in the area. He'd know she'd gotten away, foiled whatever plans he had for her. He should've been worried about the plans she'd had for *him*.

She removed her Glock from her jacket pocket and placed it on the console. She swung out of the parking lot, her tires spewing gravel, squealing and fishtailing as they hit the asphalt.

Her breathing didn't return to normal until she saw the lights of Marysville ahead. A few sets of headlights crawled along the mostly empty streets where a couple of fast-food joints glowed with a warm welcome for late-night noshers. Her stomach growled, but the last thing she needed was greasy food before turning in. The food on the plane was bad enough.

She pulled into the guest parking lot of the hotel, pocketed her weapon and slid from her rental car. She stomped her feet before entering the lobby, dislodging some dirt and debris from her shoes.

Crossing the lobby to the elevator, she waved at the front-desk clerk.

His eyes widened, as he lifted his hand. "Are you okay, Ms....?"

"Brunetti." She slowed her pace. "I'm fine. Why do you ask?"

"It's just…" His face flushed, as he seemed incapable of completing a sentence. He patted the top of his head.

She reached up to her hair, which had come loose from her ponytail, and felt leaves and a small twig among the strands. As she combed her fingers through her rat's nest, she smiled at the clerk. "Just doing a little exploring in the woods. Might've gotten carried away."

The young man hunched forward on the counter, looked both ways and cupped a hand at the side of his mouth. "You might want to be careful in the woods at night. A woman was murdered there several months ago, and the cops haven't caught the killer."

A shiver ran up her back, despite this being

old news to her. "I'll be careful. Thanks for the warning."

She made a beeline for the elevator without turning around and stabbed the button several times. When she got to her room, she studied her reflection in the full-length mirror. She rubbed a smudge of dirt from her cheek and picked a few more twigs from her hair. Then she shrugged out of her dirty jacket, fell on top of the bed and toed off her sneakers, still caked with mud.

Had she almost just shot a man in the woods for shining a flashlight in her face? She'd been somewhere else when he'd come upon her, but an excuse like that wouldn't fly with the local police. It also wouldn't help her find out what happened to Katie fourteen years ago.

And she had every intention of putting that mystery to bed—even if it cost her her job... and her sanity.

THE FOLLOWING MORNING, Michael made it to the lab with a lot less confidence—and a lot less sleep—than he'd intended. He'd been prepared to attack this meeting with Special Agent Brunetti with all systems humming, and he'd barely made it out of the house today with matching socks.

The encounter with the woman in the woods last night had rattled him. The rumors of his guilt were still circulating, and now, someone had caught him returning to the scene of the crime. What had he been thinking going back there? Would she report him to the police? He hadn't done anything wrong, except for thinking she was his wife, Raine, for one crazy minute.

He must've done something, though. Lunged at her. Reached for her. Blinded her with the flashlight. He'd scared her, and she'd taken off like a scared rabbit. All she'd left behind was the scent of roses.

He'd wanted to explain, soothe her fears, but going after her would've made everything worse. He'd taken off soon after he heard her car start up. At least she hadn't called the police on him— not that he knew of, anyway.

Nicole appeared in his office doorway. "Are you ready for the meeting?"

"As ready as I'll ever be. Are you and the other department heads prepared?" He stuffed the file he'd been blindly staring at into his bag and pushed back from his chair.

"I think so. I mean, most of us weren't even at the lab when the…discrepancies occurred. Not sure what the FBI expects from us now." Nicole stepped away from the door as he approached.

"They expect cooperation and for us to open our files to them. I think we can all do that. It's not like any of our jobs are on the line over this corruption." He turned and locked his office door behind him. With the FBI in the house, now was the time to follow security procedures to the letter.

Nicole tucked an errant curl behind her ear as she took the lead to the conference room. "Everyone keeps saying corruption. Maybe it was just mismanagement. Maybe they weren't that good at their jobs."

"Could be." Michael shrugged. "It's not up to us to figure that out. We'll leave it up to Special Agent Brunetti to make the conclusions after his investigation."

The department heads had already gathered in the conference room, and Michael scanned the faces for the FBI agent. He grabbed one of the chairs at the head of the table, his back to the door, and connected his laptop to the projector. As he brought up the presentation on his computer, the mumbling in the room ceased, and he glanced over his shoulder at an attractive woman poised at the door, her brown hair pulled back from her face, accentuating a pair of high cheekbones and intelligent, brownish-gold eyes.

His gaze took in her olive-green suit and smart laptop case slung over one shoulder, and the truth smacked him in the face. Special Agent Nat Brunetti was a female—all woman, as a matter of fact.

He schooled the surprise from his face. He couldn't be accused of sexism. If he hadn't seen the first name of the special agent, he wouldn't have made any assumptions about her gender.

Standing up, he extended his hand. "Special Agent Brunetti, I'm Dr. Michael Wilder. Welcome to our lab. We look forward to assisting you."

Her full lips twitched, but she took his hand in a firm grip. "Good to meet you, Dr. Wilder. Thanks for the welcome, and you can call me Natalie or Nat."

"Please, call me Michael." He flung his arm to the side. "We'll go around the room, and everyone can introduce themselves to you and say a few words about their department. Only Dr. Volosin from the DNA lab is missing, as he's at a conference out of town. His assistant manager, Dr. Rachelle Butler, is representing the lab today."

Most of his staff had friendly words and smiles for Agent Brunetti, but the welcome wagon hit a rut when it came to Lou Gray, who oversaw vehicle evidence. Lou scowled at Natalie from beneath a pair of bushy eyebrows. "Are you Fibbies trying to disrupt our work here? Point the finger for mistakes made years ago?"

Natalie placed her fingertips on the table and leaned forward. "I assure you, Lou, that's not my job. If mistakes were made, and it looks as if they were, we want to make sure they don't happen again—here or at any other forensics lab. This isn't a search-and-destroy mission."

Lou nodded, but he didn't seem entirely convinced. He'd been working at this lab at the time of the anomalies, so he was probably feeling more threatened than most.

The rest of the introductions went more quickly and less prickly, and the meeting went even faster than Michael had anticipated. Natalie—he refused to call her Nat now—didn't ask a lot of questions, but the ones she did come up with were pertinent and precise. She also managed to put everyone at ease and establish an air of camaraderie in the room, notwithstanding Lou's hesitancy.

He could do this. They all could. They were on the same team and wanted the same thing. The FBI had sent one of their best and brightest.

Natalie deferred to Michael to wrap up the meeting, and as his team filed out, they all said a few words to Natalie, asked a few questions. His grumpy staff had sprouted halos in the past hour, all on their best behavior. Even Lou managed a smile on his way out. This audit would be a breeze.

As Natalie chatted with the last of the department heads, Michael closed out his presentation and disconnected his laptop from the projector. When he and Natalie were alone, he tapped on the conference table. "You can set up shop in this room during the audit. Lots of room to spread out with an available projector for presentations, if needed. Or I can get an office, if you prefer."

She took a turn around the room, brushing past him. "Are you sure you don't need this meeting space? I would prefer it, but not if I'm inconveniencing your lab. I'm already putting them out."

He caught a whiff of Natalie's perfume when she swept past him, and he tilted his head. Had Raine worn that scent? Did his sister? He cleared his throat. "Putting them out? After that meeting, I think you have them wrapped around your finger."

"I may have to tiptoe around Lou." Crossing her arms, she wedged her hip against the table. "Otherwise, I had strict orders from my boss to fit in and make this as painless as possible for all of you. We know these anomalies aren't the fault of you or your staff."

"Ah, so it's all an act?" He hitched his bag over his shoulder.

"Does it really matter? I'm here to do a job, and I'll do whatever it takes to get it done properly." Her fingers curled into the silky material of her pale yellow blouse. She'd shrugged off her jacket a few minutes into the meeting, which hadn't taken away from her professionalism at all.

And she was a professional, although he was no longer convinced about her sincerity.

He turned toward the door. "It doesn't matter to me. As long as you don't ruffle feathers while you're here, you'll have the complete cooperation of my staff."

She made a move behind him. "I didn't mean to offend you. Your department heads are wonderful and seem like a competent group. I know we won't have any issues at all."

As he reached the door, the smell of her perfume wafted over him again, and he inhaled the scent of roses. He stopped short and spun around. "You."

Her eyes widened, and she rose from the desk slowly. "What?"

Reaching behind him, he pushed the door to the conference room closed with a snap. A muscle ticked in his jaw as he saw her eyes dart over his shoulder at the closed door, her frame stiffening.

She asked, "What are you doing?"

"It was you in the woods last night on the Devil's Edge Trail. It was you who accused me of murdering my wife."

Chapter Three

Natalie froze. Her gaze shifted to the window that looked out onto the lab, its blinds firmly drawn. She licked her dry lips as she gave her attention to the man in front of her. His height. His frame. His deep voice. The stranger from the trail.

"I—I…" She covered her mouth with her hand. How could she explain to him that she hadn't been accusing him of murdering his wife? How could she explain that for one frantic minute in a haze from the past, she thought he was the man who'd chased her and Katie through the woods, snatching Katie and taking her away forever?

He folded his arms across his broad chest and settled his back against the door. A vein throbbed in his forehead. "Are you going to tell me that you weren't on the Devil's Edge Trail last night around ten o'clock and that you didn't tell me that you weren't going to let me kill you like I'd killed her?"

Her cheeks flamed with heat. Is that what she'd said? She bit down on her lower lip and tasted blood. Her tongue darted to the droplet and licked it off. "I was there, but I didn't know that was you out on the trail. I couldn't see your face. The light was in my eyes. And I-I don't remember what I said. You frightened me, and I yelled out, but I certainly don't remember saying those words. Why would I? I didn't even know that was you out there, and even if I did, I wouldn't be accusing you of murdering your wife."

He blinked. His black, sooty lashes sweeping over his startling blue eyes for a second. He rubbed his jaw and took a deep breath. The vein stopped pulsing. "You yelled *something* at me."

She gave him a jerky nod. "Yes. Yes, I did. I'm sorry. You startled me. I yelled something, but I don't remember what. I certainly didn't accuse you of murder. Look, I know what happened to your wife and I'm sorry, but I read you were cleared. You wouldn't be running this lab if you hadn't been."

The volcano that seemed to have been building in his body dissipated without an explosion. He ran a hand through his inky black hair and shook his head. "I apologize. I must've misinterpreted what you said. I saw a woman in front of me, afraid, and yeah, that's what I imagined you said."

Natalie's shoulders dropped. He believed her.

He'd put it down to his own fevered imagination…instead of hers. "That's ridiculous that we met that way. What are the odds? Talk about your bad first impressions."

His rather stern mouth quirked into a lopsided grin, and her heart skipped a beat. "I've been on edge, and I was an idiot aiming that flashlight in your face in the dark. Anyone would be startled."

"My own actions weren't exactly measured." She flicked her hair off her shoulder. "Why don't we get back on even footing here and go out to lunch? My treat, or at least the FBI's."

"Sounds good. Let me make some meeting notes first, and you can get set up in here." He opened the door and paused. "Contact Felicia, our admin assistant, if you need anything in the way of office supplies or printers or software log-ins. She'll set you up."

"I'll do that. Thanks." She lifted her hand and waved, as much to send him off as to clear the remaining tension from the conference room. Despite her ridiculous explanation and his ready acceptance of it, strands of that tension still vibrated in the air.

She clicked the door closed behind him and sank into a chair at the conference table. She folded her arms on top of the cool mahogany and buried her face in the crook of her elbow. How could she have been so careless? So…emotional?

She didn't want anyone to recognize her as the teen who'd been with Katie Fellows when she'd disappeared—least of all, Michael Wilder, her contact at the lab. He had to believe she was here to audit the historical evidence of his lab, which was bad enough. But she'd just about pulled it off with that meeting—all jovial camaraderie, all "let's work together as a team," all "no blame here."

They'd bought it. Ate it up. Even Wilder. She raised her head from her arms and tightened her ponytail. That name suited him, with his dark good looks and barely suppressed fury.

Had he become furious enough with his wife—almost ex-wife—to off her? He had been cleared, people had seen him elsewhere at the time, but people lied all the time to protect others.

She moved to the end of the table and plopped down in the chair she'd been previously occupying. She flipped open her laptop and opened a new document. Might as well get a list of supplies and items going for Felicia.

Her head snapped up, and she narrowed her eyes at the blinds covering the conference-room windows. How had Michael identified her as the woman from Devil's Edge Trail? She doubted he could've seen her any clearer than she'd seen him with that beam of light in her face.

She drummed her thumbs against the edge of her keyboard. She'd have to watch herself around him. The man might have a hair-trigger temper, but a keen intelligence added fire to those blue eyes…and she'd felt the heat all the way down to her toes.

MICHAEL FINISHED THE last of his notes on the meeting this morning and drained the dregs of his coffee. He'd cut way back on caffeine and tended to nurse his one cup of coffee until the cold, bitter last sip.

He saved his file with a tap and leaned back in his chair, massaging his temples. Maybe he needed to cut back even more after this morning's embarrassing outburst.

He'd just accused the FBI agent assigned to investigate his lab of calling him a killer—in the woods, in the middle of the night.

Steepling his fingers, he rested his chin on the apex. What the hell was Special Agent Natalie Brunetti doing on Devil's Edge Trail at ten o'clock at night? She'd never clarified her presence there and he'd been too flustered and ready to accept her explanation to ask.

Why didn't she mention the encounter this morning? If it was true that she hadn't recognized him, why wouldn't she talk about a frightening meeting with a strange man in the woods? Unless she didn't want anyone to know she'd been on that trail, presumably her first day in town.

Did the FBI have some ulterior motive in sending Brunetti out here? Were they trying to pin Raine's murder on him, after all? FBI agent arrives in Marysville and goes out to the scene of his wife's homicide her first night in town. What are the odds?

Maybe she did recognize him. Maybe she was expecting him. Maybe she was hoping to rattle him.

His head jerked up at the sharp rap on his door. Natalie's fake smile didn't even reach her whiskey-colored eyes. He pasted one on to rival hers. "Lunchtime already?"

"I know. We must've both been working hard for the time to pass so quickly." She clasped her hands loosely in front of her. "Are you ready for lunch? I can come back later."

"I'm starving." He pushed back from his desk, his chair banging the wall behind him, and Natalie jumped. She had that look again from the woods, as if she was ready to bolt. "Do you mind walking? There are quite a few lunch spots near the lab, and 'd like to stretch my legs."

"That sounds perfect, as long as it doesn't rain."

"Around these parts, that's always a gamble." He reached for the compact umbrella he kept in

his desk drawer. "You always need to be prepared for rain."

"Don't I know it. I mean, so I've heard, but
that's why it's so lush and green. It's a good
trade-off, don't you think?" She stepped away
from the door as he grabbed his jacket.

He was thinking a lot of things, none of which
he was about to share with her. "I like it, but then
I grew up in the desert. Give me another twenty
years here, and I might grow to hate it."

Natalie's eyes widened but she nodded, as if
she knew exactly what he meant.

As they walked through the lobby, Michael
jerked his thumb toward the security guard behind the desk. "Do you want to borrow an umbrella, just in case? Might be better than the two
of us trying to squeeze beneath this one."

The thought of sharing an umbrella with him
seemed to seal the deal for her. "That's probably
a good idea. I'll have to buy one while I'm out
here and remember to keep it with me."

Michael detoured to the security station.
"Sam, do you have an umbrella our guest can
borrow?"

"Sure do." Sam gestured toward Natalie, while
nudging a wire basket filled with multicolored
umbrellas with the toe of his shoe. "Take your
pick, ma'am."

"Thanks, Sam." Natalie hunched over the selection and picked a dark green compact umbrella. "This one should work."

Michael glanced at the large tote bag as she tucked the umbrella inside. Was this supposed to be a working lunch? He planned to get a little work in, but probably not the kind she intended.

As he ushered her out the front door, he glanced at the gray sky, still too light for rain. "Sandwiches for lunch okay, or do you prefer something more substantial?"

"Sandwiches will work, as long as I can get a Diet Coke." She rubbed her forehead with her knuckles. "I'm just beginning to feel a little jet lag. I think I'm going to need some caffeine to get through the afternoon."

"They have about a million types of soda at this place. You know those self-serve machines with every conceivable choice. Sorry, this is not a high-end joint."

"Do I look like I need high-end?" She tapped her chest, her silk blouse just visible beneath the expensive-looking dark green jacket that matched the umbrella she selected, a Burberry raincoat over top. He'd recognize those buttons anywhere.

He shrugged. "I've been out to DC before. You Fibbies do things a little differently back there."

"I assure you. We do eat sandwiches at places with self-serve soda machines." She tipped her head back and sniffed the air like a native. "What do you think? Rain?"

"I think we're safe today, but all bets are off tonight." He steered her toward the entrance to the Fantastic Café, its blue-and-white awning over the door faded from too many rainstorms.

The restaurant buzzed with activity, and he put his lips close to her ear, that rose scent tickling his nose. "I see a waitress clearing off a table by the window. I'll grab that while you get in line to order."

"Sure." She shuffled to the back of the line, the color on her cheeks heightened.

Had he gotten too close? Too familiar? If he hoped to get any information out of Natalie, he'd have to find the right balance with her. She was skittish and falsely friendly at the same time.

He reached the table just as Wendy scooped up her tip. "Can I stake a claim to this table, Wendy?"

"It's all yours, Michael. Any of the gang with you?" She stood on her tiptoes and surveyed the line at the counter.

"Nope. Someone from another agency doing some work at the lab."

"Drop your coat, and I'll make sure nobody sits here…or steals your coat." She patted his arm. "How's Ivy?"

"She's good, thanks. My sister is still here."

Some people in town had eyed him with suspicion this past year, but never Wendy. She had his back.

As Wendy walked away, he shed his coat and placed it on one of the chairs at the table. Then he joined Natalie one place away from the counter.

Pointing at the menu posted behind the registers, he asked, "See anything you like?"

"Do you recommend the tuna melts? I haven't had one of those in a hot minute."

"Everything's good here. I'm having the turkey club and homemade potato chips, which are way better than the fries."

"Sold." When it was Natalie's turn, she placed their order and held up the plastic number the cashier gave her. "You can put this on the table. I'll get our drinks."

"Root beer for me. Just the plain stuff, no vanilla or cherry or whatever else they have." He held out his hand. "Do you want me to take your bag back to the table?"

She clamped her arm against the bag, pinning it to her body. "That's okay. I'm used to lugging it around."

He watched her thread her way through the line still queuing up at the counter before turning toward the table. She had an edginess to her. He knew a lot of cops who displayed wariness. He figured the FBI must be the same.

He set the number on the edge of the table and sat on the chair next to his coat. As he pulled some napkins from the dispenser, Natalie returned with their sodas.

"You weren't kidding about that soda machine. There were flavors I never even heard of." She put his paper cup in front of him, along with a straw. "Plain old root beer."

"And how about you?" He tapped the side of her cup with his straw. "Did you take a walk on the wild side?"

"Plain old Diet Coke for me, but I might do a refill with the Zesty Blood Orange flavor." She hung her bag on the back of the chair next to her and sat in the one across from him.

They spent the next few minutes poking straws into their drinks, grabbing napkins and chatting about the weather, but Michael had no intention of wasting this lunch on small talk. He needed answers from Special Agent Brunetti.

Once their food arrived and he gave her time to eat, he held up a potato chip. "Was I right?"

"So good. Everything is."

"You know—" he wiped his hands on a napkin and balled it up in his fist "—we had that heated moment in the conference room when I accused you of accusing me, but I never did get around to asking you why you were in the forest at night in the first place. On that trail."

Natalie swallowed her bite of food, covered the bottom half of her face with a napkin and then took a sip of her drink, each movement measured and precise.

Michael could see the wheels turning in her head.

She repeated, "On that trail."

"It's called the Devil's Edge Trail. If you keep following it deeper into the woods, it ends with a drop-off into a canyon. Really dangerous at night if you don't know the terrain. Why were you there?" He took a big bite of his sandwich, as if her answer was only of mild interest.

She rolled her eyes to the ceiling and snapped her fingers. "That's why it looked so different from the picture. I was on the wrong trail. I was trying to find the Bright Star Trail."

He decided to employ her delay tactics, and took his time patting his mouth with a napkin and sipping his root beer. "Bright Star is the opposite direction. Why would you be taking that trail...or any trail at that time of night?"

A potato chip snapped in her fingers, and she dropped the pieces onto her plate. "One of the cold cases—Lizzy Johnson. Hikers discovered her body on Bright Star. After flying all day, I got restless and decided to check out one of the scenes."

At night? He left the words unsaid and shrugged. "Yeah, opposite direction from that campsite."

A smile twisted her lips, and her dark eyes drilled into him. "I guess I could ask you the same thing. What were you doing on Devil's Edge Trail at night?"

Unlike her, he didn't feel any need to lie. She already knew his wife had been murdered and that he had been the prime suspect for a while. He pushed away his plate and folded his arms on the table. "I often go to Devil's Edge at night, although not as often as I used to."

Her nostrils flared, as if she was sensing danger, but she pursued it. "That specific trail? Why do you go there at night?"

"That's where my wife was murdered."

Chapter Four

Natalie couldn't breathe for a second. Michael's wife was murdered in the same place where Katie disappeared? How had she not known this?

Why was he visiting the scene of his wife's murder? If he was innocent? She became aware a few seconds too late that her mouth was hanging open.

"I-I'm sorry. I didn't know that." She cleared her throat. "Do you mind if I ask you why you go there? Isn't it upsetting?"

Spreading his hands, he said, "I'm not sure I can answer that question. I think at the beginning I went hoping to find some overlooked clue."

She could relate to that. She was hoping to find some overlooked clue in Katie's disappearance...fourteen years later. She found herself nodding.

Seemingly encouraged, he continued. "I wanted answers, not just to clear myself, but for my daughter."

Second whammy in one lunch. Michael had a daughter? "I didn't realize you had a daughter. Her mother's death must've been traumatic for her...and you."

"It's been—" he shook his cup, rattling the ice "—confusing for her. She's young. Just turned two. But it's not the first time she's been without her mother."

He pressed his lips together, clamping down on any more confidences.

Their conversation had taken a detour she hadn't expected. Had Michael, or anyone else, made the connection between Raine Wilder's homicide and the disappearance of Katie Fellows fourteen years ago? Not that she actually believed the same person was responsible. Too much time had passed, and the victims had different profiles—one was an older, married woman with a child, and the other was a carefree teenager.

Plenty of wooded trails and dark forests and deep canyons surrounded Marysville, and crime scenes dotted these areas. It wouldn't be unusual for different killers to zero in on the same spots for their evil deeds.

She sniffed and dabbed her nose with a napkin.

"Sorry. I didn't mean to put a damper on lunch. I haven't been great company in a long time." He jabbed a finger at her cup. "Do you want that refill now?"

"Please." She gave the cup to him, her fingertips brushing his hand.

"Zesty Blood Orange?"

She shook her head. "No. Just the regular Diet Coke. I kinda lost my curiosity."

Ten minutes later, they walked into the lobby of the lab. Natalie held up the umbrella. "Didn't open it once."

Sam peeked out the window. "You'd better hold on to it. Once the wind kicks up, it'll bring the rain clouds with it."

Pointing to the ceiling, Michael said, "You can smell it already."

Natalie asked, "Are you sure about the umbrella?"

"That one's been around for a while. If someone comes looking for it, I'll send them your way." Sam winked.

"Thanks, Sam." She followed Michael up the stairs, and they stopped at the top, where their paths diverged.

"I forgot to ask if you got everything you needed today. You good in the conference room?"

"It's perfect. Room to spread out. I'm going to need it, as I'll probably be dragging some boxes up from the evidence room."

"That conference room will afford you plenty

of space for that." He turned slightly, running a hand through his hair. "Thanks for lunch and sorry it got so heavy."

"I think that's unavoidable in our line of work and thanks for the recommendation. Lunch was delicious, and I feel like I can fight off this jet lag for another three hours." She shook her cup, still half-filled with soda, at him.

"We're all at your disposal. Let any of us know if there's anything else you need."

She held up her finger. "There is something. I need access to the lab's personnel records—hard copies or online—for the past fifteen years or so. I need to compile a database of the lab employees who were here during those years when the evidence went wonky."

"That's one way of putting it. We don't have those records here, but I can call Seattle for you and request them. I'm guessing they're all online, so it would be a matter of giving you access to the personnel program. I don't even have that. Human Resources for the Washington State Patrol would be responsible. But I know the HR manager. I'll give her a call."

"Thanks, Michael."

He strode off to the left to catch up with one of his lab managers, and Natalie turned right toward the conference room. She stumbled to a stop when she reached the door, which was open a crack. She thought she'd closed it firmly, but then probably not everyone knew she'd set up shop here. Maybe Felicia could print her a temporary sign she could tape to the door.

An empty coat-tree sat in the corner, and Natalie hung up her raincoat and newfound umbrella. She dropped her oversize bag at her feet.

As she flipped open her laptop, she reached for the mouse on her right. Her fingers skimmed across the empty mousepad, and she turned her head to find the mouse off the pad and out of reach.

She screwed up her mouth on one side. She preferred using a mouse to the touchpad on the laptop and always brought it and the mousepad with her when she traveled. She'd left it on the mousepad. Had someone been in the conference room to clean up?

Her gaze shifted to the credenza against the wall, and she blew out a breath. Someone had cleared out the pitcher of water, the coffee pot, the tray of muffins and cups that had been there during the meeting. Felicia, or whoever had cleaned up, probably dusted a few crumbs from the table, too, and repositioned her mouse.

As she reached for her mouse, Dr. Butler tapped on the door. "Sorry to interrupt you. Just wanted to tell you that if you want to interview me before Dr. Volosin comes back later in the week, I can provide you with anything you need."

"Thank you. Dr. Volosin isn't returning until the end of the week?"

"That's right. He's helping with a case down in Portland right now." Dr. Butler glanced over her shoulder. "You might find me a little easier to work with than him, anyway."

Raising her eyebrows, Natalie asked, "Another Lou Gray?"

Dr. Butler flicked back her long, beaded braids. "Dr. Volosin has also been at this forensics lab for a long time, like Lou, so they were both here during the cold-case time periods."

"Got it." That's exactly why Natalie wanted to speak to Dr. Volosin instead of the amenable Dr. Butler. The more outwardly contentious the interview, the greater possibility of getting to the truth.

As Dr. Butler turned to leave, she paused in the doorjamb. "I'm glad you're here, Agent Brunetti. Michael knows his stuff, but he can't always be everywhere at once."

Dr. Butler closed the door behind her before Natalie had a chance to ask her what she meant. She made a mental note to definitely talk to Dr. Butler before her boss returned.

Natalie returned her attention to her computer and accessed the file she'd started before lunch.

She'd created a database of the cold cases she'd been sent to investigate and had set one up for her own personal investigation, as well.

The shadow database mimicked the official one. She'd investigate the evidence for both sets in the same way, using the same methods. She didn't know why her department had left off those two cases, including Katie's, but it hadn't been her place to suggest which cold cases she'd investigate and which ones she wouldn't. She didn't want to draw attention to her interest in those cases.

The fact that Michael's wife had met her demise in the same location that Katie disappeared had shocked her. She'd made a habit over the years of searching for Devil's Edge Trail in relation to homicides to keep tabs on any other crimes in the vicinity. She'd missed Raine Wilder's murder.

She and Michael had been in that location last night for their own ghoulish reasons. Of course, he'd been willing to reveal his motive, while she'd kept silent. Nobody needed to know her ulterior motives for being here. Nobody needed to know her connection to this area.

She'd studied a few of the faces in the cafe at lunch. Of course, she remembered the restaurant from her teen years here. She'd even remembered the homemade potato chips. Sometimes

she and her friends, including Katie, would pop
into Fantastic Cafe on their way home from
school just to pick up an order of chips. They'd
hold the little brown bags with the grease spots
leaking through the waxy paper cupped in one
hand, while plucking out chips and popping
them into their mouths. The best part was licking the salt off her fingers. She'd needed all her
concentration at lunch today not to do the same.
Lost in the memory, a smile tugged at her lips.

The two other girls in their clique, Bella and
Megyn, had avoided her after the incident. Had
she reminded them of their shared loss of Katie
Or had they just figured she was bad news and
toxic company? It had been her idea, after all,
to go into the woods at night.

Bella and Megyn hadn't joined them that fate-
ful night after what had happened on their previous outing into the woods. Natalie shivered.
That should've been a warning to all of them,
but she and Katie liked to push the envelope.

Her email notification pinged and she clicked
on the new message. She scanned the email from
the Washington State Patrol HR department. Michael must've gotten right on her request for the
personnel records. The email included a link to
their employee records and a temporary user-
name and password for Natalie.

As she clicked on the link, an alarm sounded

in the building. She half rose from her chair and peered through the blinds. People began emerging from offices and work areas, heading toward the stairs.

She jumped up when someone knocked on the conference-room door. Before she had a chance to answer it, Michael poked his head inside the room.

He said, "It's a fire drill. I'm sure it's just a test, but we have monitors, and they'll report any infractions of the rules. That means everyone out of the building."

"I guess I could use a break, anyway." She started to gather her files and reach for her bag, but Michael put his hands up.

"We're meant to leave everything behind. Just grab your coat. Security will be watching the front door while we're out in the parking lot."

Natalie snatched her coat from the tree and followed Michael out the door, joining the stream of people descending the stairs. As she stuffed her arms in her coat, she said, "I hope the rain hasn't started. I also left my umbrella behind."

"We're good for now." They surged through the open front doors with the rest of the lab employees, and Michael put a hand on her back. "We have to gather all the way across the parking lot, even if it's a drill."

"I work for the government, too. This is nothing new to me." They joined the others under some trees, on the other side of the parking lot. "Thanks for contacting HR so quickly. They already sent me a link to the personnel database and a log-in."

"We have strict instructions to play nice with the FBI—any outside agency, really. There are too many cold cases on the books that show a lack of cooperation between agencies. In a lot of instances, that lack of cooperation is why they're cold cases."

Natalie said, "It's good to hear departments like yours are putting emphasis on working with outside agencies. I'll be sending good reports back to my supervisor."

He lifted one eyebrow. "Can the FBI claim the same?"

"What does that mean?" A gust of wind kicked up, bringing the scent of rain with it, and she glanced at the clouds scudding across the sky.

"Come on. The FBI is notorious for playing its cards close to the vest. The Feds expect everyone else to turn over all their stuff, but they keep a lot of information to themselves."

She put a finger to her lips.

It wasn't the FBI that was keeping secrets from Michael, but her secrets wouldn't matter to him—except the one where her friend disappeared from the same trail where his wife was murdered.

A horn blared from the building, and people began shuffling across the parking lot. She cranked her head back and forth, scanning the area. "That's it? The fire engines didn't even show up."

"Could've been a planned exercise. We also have active-shooter drills and shelter in place. I'm not sure what warrants a visit from the fire department, but I don't think the powers that be want to keep us out here any longer." He held out a hand, palm down. "I just felt a big, fat raindrop."

"Perfect timing." Natalie hugged her coat around her frame.

By the time they entered the lobby, the skies had opened, and water spattered the windows. Most people who worked on the second floor avoided the elevator, so Natalie climbed the stairs with the other lab workers, nodding at a few familiar faces from the meeting earlier in the day.

When she reached the conference room, she shoved open the door and removed her coat. After hanging it up, she took her place in front of her laptop and returned to the email with the log-in information for the employee database.

She cross-checked the database with the dates of her cold cases with the missing or corrupted evidence, including Katie and Alma's cases, which were similar Several of the same people had worked all the cases, which didn't surprise her. A few of those employees still held positions at the lab.

The crimes were clustered in a ten-year span. Ten years at the same forensics lab didn't jump out at her as unusual at all. Lab rats had to put in the time to be considered specialists in their fields. Being designated a specialist came with its own perks and bragging rights.

She noticed a few people packing up and leaving the office. She'd decided to keep the blinds open on the windows of the conference room. She didn't want anyone to think she was hiding anything from them…even though she was. Appearances sweetened the path to acceptance.

She saved her files and chugged some tepid water from her glass this morning. She'd accomplished a lot today, not the least of which was getting to know Michael Wilder a little better. He'd opened up to her more than she'd expected.

Part of being transparent was not working alone after hours, so she logged off her computer and started packing. She reached down for the bag at her feet and opened it to slide in the laptop.

When she glanced inside, her heart stopped. Her two files, Katie's and Alma's, were gone. She dragged the bag to the table and spread it open, ridiculously checking corners that couldn't possibly accommodate two file folders.

She slumped in her chair. Someone in this office had stolen those files...and they'd orchestrated a fake fire drill to do it.

Chapter Five

Michael picked up his cell phone and tapped his sister's name. Pathetic that he had to call to tell her he'd be home in time for dinner tonight… for a change.

Molly answered on the first ring. "Don't tell me you're gonna be late again. I actually cooked dinner. You know, like I chopped some onions, peppers and garlic, and turned on the stove and everything."

"Sounds like spaghetti sauce."

"Duh, it's the only thing I know how to cook, except eggs—not that I'm above having eggs for dinner."

Michael smiled into the phone. When his mother had suggested Molly come out and help with Ivy, he thought she was joking. His sister didn't have a single housekeeping bone in her body, but it turned out Mom was right. Ivy didn't need housekeeping or home-cooked meals or orderly toy bins. She needed attention and love and fun, and Molly could supply all those things in spades.

Michael coughed. "I'm calling to let you know I'll be home by six. I was going to take you two out for pizza tonight, but if you went through the trouble of cooking, I'm going to make it worth your while."

"You might wanna keep that pizza on standby, just in case things in the kitchen go south. See you at six."

When Molly ended the call, Michael cupped the phone between his hands and took a deep breath. Maybe it was time to turn the page, move on. Verbally explaining to Natalie today why he was visiting the location of his wife's murder made him realize how fruitless it was…and how ridiculous it all sounded—about as ridiculous as Natalie's explanation about taking the wrong trail.

She presented herself as a thorough professional. No way would she mix up those two trails. So what was she doing on Devil's Edge at night?

A knock at his door refocused his attention, and he glanced up to see the very person from his thoughts, as if he'd conjured her. "Wrapping it up? Hope you had a productive first day."

Leaning against his doorjamb, she said, "I did. Got a lot of work done. That fire drill was kind of annoying and broke my concentration, but I guess these types of systems need to be tested. Was it a test?"

"What?" He slipped his phone into his pocket and logged off his computer.

"The fire drill. Was that a planned test, or…?" She shifted the bag on her shoulder, grasping the strap with both hands.

"I don't have a clue. The alarm sounds, and I head outside." He shrugged. "Do you want to lodge a complaint or something?"

"Maybe."

He glanced up from shoving his laptop into his bag. She'd sounded serious about that, but she had a smile on her face. Or was that a grimace? "If you're serious about it, I suppose you can contact the building manager, but I don't think it would do any good. You know these government agencies. We play by the rules."

"Oh, I understand if it was a test, but not if it was a prank. That's unacceptable."

"A prank?" He blinked. "You mean, like someone pulled the alarm for laughs? I hope you haven't gotten the impression that I foster an environment here that would encourage that."

"No, no. I guess not. Maybe an accident." She smoothed her hair back with one hand. "I guess I'm just annoyed that it broke my concentration, but I did create a couple of databases that are going to be very useful. Did you realize that a few of your current lab employees were around during the time that evidence was…mishandled?"

"Yeah, I'm aware." He pushed back from his desk and stood up. He told Molly he'd be home on time tonight, and he'd stick to that. "I don't have to tell you to tread carefully there. Nobody wants to be grilled like a criminal."

"We just want to find out what happened to the evidence and make some progress toward solving these cold cases. Everyone… The families deserve answers and justice, if possible."

"Justice is always possible." He flicked off his office light, and Natalie stepped back into the hallway. "If you need some recommendations for dinner tonight, I'd be happy to text you a list of places."

"I'm okay. I might just wander around the downtown area and see what looks good. My hotel is walking distance."

"Good idea. You'll find something."

They walked outside together, and Natalie hesitated before she turned in the opposite direction in the parking lot. Should he have invited her to dinner? *Bad idea.* He didn't want to mix business with pleasure. Because he had to admit, he found the company of Special Agent Natalie Brunetti pleasurable.

By the time he got home, the smell of garlic saturated the air, and his mouth watered. He came up behind his sister in the kitchen and tapped her on the shoulder.

She jumped. "You scared me."

"You didn't hear me come through the door?" He skirted her and dipped a spoon into the bubbling tomato sauce, blew the steam away and slurped up the sauce. "Mmm, good."

"Maybe you should get a watchdog to warn me." She jerked her head over her shoulder and clapped a hand over her mouth. "I'm sorry."

He dropped the spoon on the counter. "Is Ivy still napping?"

"She was a little cranky. I put her down for a nap, so she'd be bright-eyed and bushy-tailed for Dada." Molly aimed her knife at a loaf of sourdough bread on a baking sheet. "Can you finish the garlic bread? I already mixed up the garlic butter and sliced the loaf. You just need to spread some butter on both sides."

"This really is a homemade dinner. You could've bought some frozen garlic bread." He stepped to the sink to wash his hands.

"I thought you needed a celebration. The FBI audit started today, right? Your prep should be over. No more long nights at the office."

"It did, and it is." He scooped a knife in the butter and slathered it on the first piece of bread.

"The prep is over, but I'm not sure my work is completely done. The agent the FBI sent out seems to be a stickler. I have a feeling she'll be asking us to jump and fetch."

"She?" Molly wiggled her eyebrows up and down. "Is she hot?"

Michael wrinkled his nose. "If you like kind-of-uptight, stand-offish, holier-than-thou women. Then she's your type."

"Not my type." Molly threw open a cupboard door, which smacked against another cupboard. "But that might be a nice change for you."

He opened his mouth to protest but snapped it shut as he caught sight of Molly's stormy face. Molly's ex-girlfriend had been just that type, a corporate lawyer who'd supported Molly as she struggled with selling her art. Molly's haphazard lifestyle had finally lost its charm for Gracie, and they broke up last year.

Holding up the baking sheet with the bread, he asked, "Ready for the oven?"

"About fifteen minutes should do it. I already preheated the oven." She took two plates and two bowls from the cupboard. "You wanna set the table?"

He slid the baking sheet onto the rack in the hot oven, and as he took the dishes from her, he heard Ivy cry out from her room. His hands tightened on the plates. Ever since her mother left, Ivy had been having a tough time waking up from sleep.

Michael almost believed that Ivy dreamed of her mother and at the moment she woke up, she remembered all over again that she was gone. Not that Raine had been a great mom to Ivy. Raine had abandoned her daughter once before when she left him. Then she'd decided in the middle of the divorce proceedings that she really did want her daughter. That's why he'd been suspect number one in her murder—they'd been fighting over custody of Ivy. No way in hell would he have allowed Ivy to live with Raine. Now, he didn't have to worry about that.

As Molly turned, Michael put a hand on her arm. "If you don't mind setting the table. I'll get her."

"Of course. She'll be thrilled to see you home for dinner. I'm just the babysitter."

Michael rubbed his sister's back. "You are her rock right now…and I think she has more fun with you."

"Nobody has ever called me a rock before—not even you." She sniffed and dabbed her nose with the back of her hand.

He moved his hand up to her neck and gave it a quick squeeze. "Mom told me you were the one to watch Ivy, so she has faith in you, as well."

That first cry was Ivy's last, so Michael poked

his head in her darkened room to make sure she was awake. She still slept in a crib. He'd been ready to move her to a toddler bed, had bought the bed and everything, but when Raine was murdered, and Ivy's development seemed to regress, he'd shoved the box into the garage. Same with the little plastic potty. He'd rather deal with diapers and have a successful run at potty training later than force the issue now.

He drank in the sight of his little girl standing in her crib, holding on to the railing and swaying back and forth to a mumbled tune. His heart swelled as he watched her, and ached a little, too. How would he be able to give her everything she needed? How would he be able to raise a daughter on his own? It had been hard enough trying to raise her with a mother like Raine—who'd been absent, self-obsessed, narcissistic—but at least Raine had loved Ivy, and Ivy had loved her mother.

A sigh escaped his lips, and Ivy jerked toward him. A smile engulfed her pixie face, and she raised her arms as she said in a singsong voice, "Daddy."

She'd recently switched back to calling him *Daddy*. *Dada* had been her baby name for him, and she'd regressed to that months ago, but now *daddy* was creeping back into her vocabulary.

That had to be a good sign, right? Hell, he'd take it.

He strode across the room and scooped her up, his hands firmly under her arms. He swung her around until her legs flew in the air behind her and her giggles turned into shrieks of laughter. Then he cuddled her close and kissed her forehead, both cheeks, her chin and her nose.

She patted his face and then repeated the same set of kisses, landing the final one on his nose. Their ritual melted his heart every time.

"Auntie Molly cooked us dinner. Spaghetti." He tucked her under one arm and spun around to the changing table, which she'd outgrown. "But first we'll get another pull-up."

Her lower lip jutted forward. "Unnywear, Daddy."

"That's right, underwear." Molly had started reintroducing the language for potty training, and Ivy seemed receptive. Maybe they'd have another go at it.

Once he had a clean pull-up in place for Ivy, he took her to the sink, and she climbed up on her step stool to wash her hands.

As she rubbed her hands under the faucet, he asked, "What happened when you went on the swings at the park today? What kinds of pictures did you paint with Auntie Molly?"

Raine's disappearance had caused Ivy's language to lag, and Michael had consulted with his psychologist friend for tips on getting her to talk more. He tried to follow through on her suggestion to ask Ivy specific questions instead of open-ended ones. It seemed to work.

Tonight, Ivy babbled on about flying on the swing, and how Molly had twisted up the chains and then released them until Ivy spun around. She was still talking about the dog she painted when they made it to the kitchen just as Molly was taking the bread out of the oven.

When Molly closed the oven door, Michael set Ivy on the floor. "Get your plate and cup from Auntie Molly and set your place at the table."

Ivy scampered to Molly and took the brightly colored plastic, partitioned plate and cup from her. On the way to the table, she poked at a picture hanging on the fridge. "Here, Daddy. Peaches."

Michael's chest tightened as he glanced at the scribbles on the page, barely making out a pair of ears, a nose and four stick legs. Ivy still remembered the dog. "That's a nice picture of Peaches, sweetie."

"Mama take Peaches." Ivy put her plate and cup on the table and climbed into her booster seat.

Their dog, Peaches, had disappeared at the same time as Raine. The babysitter had reported that Raine had taken Peaches for a walk after visiting Ivy. He'd thought it cruel of her at the time to take the dog and not return her, but when those hikers discovered Raine's body on the trail, Peaches was nowhere to be found. He hadn't seen the dog since.

Raine had been visiting Ivy that night while he'd been at work. Natasha, Ivy's babysitter, had called him as soon as Raine showed up at the house, but he didn't think there would be any harm in Raine visiting her daughter for a few hours. When she left with Peaches, Raine had told Natasha she was taking her for a walk and would bring her back before Michael got home.

Natasha had freaked out when Raine turned up dead. He never did figure out if Natasha believed him guilty of the murder, but she couldn't work in the house anymore. So Ivy lost her mother, her babysitter and the dog all at once.

Ivy had talked about the dog when she first disappeared but hadn't mentioned Peaches in a while. He didn't know if this was a good sign or more regression. He'd ask the shrink.

Ivy's chatter at the dinner table *was* a good sign, though. And as Molly and Ivy had a spaghetti-slurping contest, he laughed so hard, things almost felt normal again.

When he tried to help his sister clean up the kitchen, she shooed him away to play with Ivy. By the time he'd colored some mermaids, built a castle with blocks, knocked it down and read a few stories, Ivy was ready for bed.

After tucking her in, he tapped on Molly's door. "You still awake?"

"C'mon in. I'm just sprucing up my profile for this dating app."

He groaned as he pushed open the door. "I don't get how you think those dating sites work."

"They work." She glanced up from her phone. "You should try it sometime. I'll help you with a profile, if you think you have any pictures where you're not scowling or brooding."

"No, thanks." Did Natalie think he was a scowler and a brooder. "Hey, I just wanted to thank you again for looking after Ivy. She seems...better."

"She's a little firecracker. I think she's starting to spark again."

He chewed his bottom lip. "Did she draw a picture of Peaches on her own, or did you ask her to do it?"

She shook her head, and her black bangs fell over her eyes. "I didn't mention Peaches, and when she drew the dog, she didn't tell me that was Peaches. In the kitchen was the first time I heard the name from her."

"Maybe it just occurred to her when she saw the picture on the fridge. Just triggered the memory of the dog."

"They never found the dog's leash or collar or…anything?" Molly tossed her phone on the bed and folded her hands in her lap.

"You mean like a dead dog in the woods?" He scratched his chin. He didn't want to tell his sister the number of times he'd been out on that trail calling Peaches's name. "Nothing, not even bones that might be hers."

Hunching her shoulders, she said, "Peaches could be a witness to murder."

"It's not like she could point out anyone in a lineup."

"Dogs are pretty smart." She tapped her head with her finger.

"You didn't know Peaches." He smacked the doorjamb. "I'm going to do some work. Thanks for dinner and cleaning up—and be careful on those dating apps."

She waved her hand in the air. "Bye. Mind your own business."

He closed her door and sank into his recliner, pulling his computer onto his lap. He flipped it open and drummed his thumbs on the keyboard. He didn't know exactly what he was looking for, or even how to start, but something in Natalie Brunetti's demeanor had set off alarm bells in his brain…and he didn't mean the way his body reacted to her. That feeling originated somewhere far south of his brain.

Sometimes her smile looked fake to him. It could just come down to an auditor trying to get on the right side of the objects of her investigation. Then there was the whole bizarre reaction to the fire drill this afternoon. She'd been digging for something. And what the hell had she been doing on Devil's Edge Trail last night? It's not a trail any stranger would just stumble on.

He launched a search engine and entered her name. A few Natalie Brunettis popped up, and he clicked on their social-media profiles. None was for his Natalie, but then, FBI agents didn't typically splash their lives in pictures across the internet.

He dug a little deeper. Maybe she'd received some awards from the FBI. Maybe she'd been a featured speaker at a conference. Maybe she'd worked a big case that had grabbed headlines. His Natalie remained elusive.

Michael balanced the laptop on the arm of the chair and went back into the kitchen. Molly had left a plate in the sink, so he rinsed off the breadcrumbs and opened the dishwasher. He rolled his eyes at the helter-skelter way his sister had loaded the dishwasher, but he'd never complain about her haphazard ways again. She was helping him bring his little girl back.

Molly had left a half a bottle of red wine on the counter, its cork shoved in the top. He'd asked his sister to avoid drinking alcohol around Ivy, and he followed his own rule. His daughter had seen enough of that in her short life.

But with Ivy sound asleep, Molly must've grabbed the opportunity to down a couple of glasses, by the looks of it, and he'd do the same. He snagged a wineglass from the top shelf of the cupboard and poured himself a healthy quantity.

He took a sip and carried the glass back to the living room. Seated once again with the computer in his lap, he ran over that first meeting with Natalie in the woods. Had he really imagined she'd said those words to him? Called him a killer?

Something about that trail had drawn Natalie into the woods after dark, and he knew it hadn't been one of the cold cases. He'd reviewed those cases before she arrived. Devil's Edge hadn't been host to one of those crime scenes…just his wife's.

His fingers hovered over the keyboard, and then he attacked it, searching for Devil's Edge Trail in Marysville, Washington. He physically shuddered when the first item on the page recounted Raine's murder. He skimmed past several more articles about her homicide until he reached the more benign links discussing the route of the trail and its flora and fauna.

Frustrated, he took a big gulp of wine. Was

Natalie out here trying to tie him to his wife's murder? Why would she waste her time? He'd been officially cleared.

He set down his glass on the end table beside him and rubbed his hands together. He flexed his fingers and came at his search from a slightly different angle. This time he searched for crimes and Devil's Edge Trail.

Of course, he had to slog through Raine's murder again, but on the next screen he stopped scrolling at a headline that mentioned the disappearance of a teen from Devil's Edge fourteen years earlier. Unlike Raine, this girl's body had never been found, and law enforcement at the time had eventually dismissed the girl, Katie Fellows, as a runaway, despite her friend's insistence that the two of them had been stalked through the woods by a strange man.

He did another search, for Katie Fellows this time, and clicked on an article that had been published at the time of her disappearance. As he read through the article, which contained a few pictures of the girls, he stumbled across the name of Katie's friend—Nat Cooper. *Nat.*

He tapped one of the photos of the accompanying article and enlarged it with his fingers, zeroing in on the face of Nat Cooper, her curly dark hair and big eyes giving him a jolt.

He fell back against the recliner and took another slug of wine. Nat Brunetti hadn't taken a wrong turn last night. She hadn't been trying to catch him in the act.

Nat Brunetti had her own reasons for returning to Marysville...and she didn't want anyone to know about them.

Chapter Six

Dishes clattered next to her, as the busboy cleared the table and collected the tip. Natalie hunched over her coffee and massaged her temple. The nightmare had hit her hard last night, and her head throbbed this morning. Instead of settling her terrors from fourteen years ago, her proximity to the scene of the crime had stoked them.

And now, someone had her files. There must be cameras in the building. If she asked security to identify the person sneaking into the conference room during the fire drill, she'd have her suspect, but then she'd have to explain what those files contained…and why.

The security guard may not know or care about the files, but it would get back to Michael, and he seemed to run that lab like a tight ship.

If Special Agent Jefferson found out about her ties to this area and her private investigation into a cold case, he'd yank her off this detail in a hot minute. She had no doubt that if Michael found out, he'd report her to Jefferson. Michael seemed cooperative, but who wanted the FBI snooping around their forensics lab?

She might've even suspected Michael of stealing the files to get some dirt on her, and he *had* insisted that she leave everything behind in the conference room, but she'd been with him for the duration of the fire drill and evacuation. He could've had someone do his dirty work while he distracted her. His employees seemed loyal to him. They'd even supported him while suspicion hung over his head about his wife's homicide.

He'd had an alibi for the time his wife disappeared, too. At work. Didn't mean he hadn't hired someone for that evil deed, either. The man had just enough smoldering anger beneath his dark, moody good looks to be a suspect.

The time on her cell phone told her to get to the lab for another day of scanning through databases, files and case records amid sidelong suspicious glances—hers not theirs. She'd be holding her breath all day waiting for that shoe to drop, that phone call from Jefferson ordering her back to DC. Because why else would anyone be interested in her files?

How did this person even know she'd had anything to hide? Hadn't she come across as professional? Cooperative? One of the boys? Someone must've seen beneath her demeanor to the desperation and deceit. The only person she'd spent any time with had been Michael.

It started with Michael.

Fifteen minutes later, she pulled into the parking lot of the lab, checked in with security with her temporary badge and jogged upstairs to her temporary office. Then she made a beeline for Michael's office.

She hovered at his open doorway before he noticed her, and she studied his face in profile as he worked at his computer. He wore his black hair swept back from his high forehead, and his hawkish nose gave him the appearance of a Roman emperor. Oh, yeah. He could command just about anyone to do anything...except his wife. And her.

It took her a second to realize he'd detected her presence and was now staring back at her, those blue eyes startlingly out of place for a Roman emperor.

Feeling her cheeks warm, she tilted up her chin. "Good morning. I wanted to ask if I can have a key to the conference room. It does have a lock on it, but I'd like a way to get back inside. I'll be bringing the case files up there today and would be nice to secure them."

He swung around to face her and steepled his fingers. "Of course. I'll get one of the guards to check on that for you. Did you have a nice evening? Jet leg?"

"Not too much. I had some food delivered to my hotel from a diner down the street and got to bed early." She left out the part where her nightmare kept her tossing and turning all night. She must have bags under her eyes if he thought she had jet lag. Should've applied more concealer.

"I'm sorry. I should've invited you to dinner on your first night…second night here. In fact, everyone in the lab should take a turn having you over for a meal." He'd crossed his arms over his chest and was watching her from half-lidded eyes in a position that hardly screamed out a welcome. Was he being sarcastic?

Her lips tightened for a second. "You're joking, right? Nobody needs to wine and dine me."

"This is Marysville, not the Beltway. We don't wine and dine. I'm talking about a home-cooked meal. My sister actually made dinner last night, and it wasn't half bad."

"Y-your sister? You live with your sister?" She didn't expect that.

"She's been out here for the past six months, helping me with my daughter." With his arms still crossed, his fingers bunched into the sleeves of his button-down shirt, crumpling the fabric.

"You're lucky to have her help."

He gave a brief nod. "Do you have any children, Nat?"

His narrowed eyes and hard jaw turned the

question into an interrogation, and she shifted from one foot to the other. And when had he started calling her *Nat*? She'd gone by her old nickname until about four years ago, but she did still sign most of her FBI correspondence as *Nat*, as she'd joined the Bureau as Nat Brunetti—and it made people think she was a man. Michael must've seen that correspondence.

She cleared her throat. "No, I don't have any children."

"Married?"

"No." Was he asking for personal reasons?

"Ever been married?"

"As a matter of fact, I *was* married, briefly." She turned away from his office. She didn't feel like telling Michael about her short, disastrous marriage that she ruined. "I can talk to security about the key to the conference room, if that's okay with you."

"Absolutely." He swung back to his computer screen. "If there's a problem, have them call me."

She went back downstairs and approached Sam behind the security desk. "Hi, Sam. I'm Natalie Brunetti. I borrowed the umbrella yesterday."

"Sure, I remember. You can keep it."

"Thanks, but I came down here to ask if you have a key to the conference room upstairs. It's my temporary office while I'm here, and I'd be more comfortable if I could lock it." She jerked her thumb toward the ceiling, as if Sam needed a reminder which direction was upstairs.

"I have that key. Let me check in the back. You can wait here."

"Thanks." She leaned against the counter while trying to frame her next request to Sam in her mind.

A few minutes later, he emerged from the office behind the counter jingling a set of keys on a silver ring. "I have two keys for that office. I'll keep one here, and you can take the other."

"Perfect."

He removed one key from the ring and dropped it into her open palm. "Just make sure you return it when you leave."

"I'll put it on my list." She dipped her hand into her purse to retrieve the key fob for her rental car. As she slid the conference room key onto the ring, she asked, "Does the lab have a lot of fire drills like the one yesterday?"

"Not like the one yesterday." He swung the ring containing the other key around his finger.

She caught her breath. "No? How was yesterday's different?"

"It wasn't planned. Took us all by surprise. I thought for a minute there might've been a real fire."

"So it was a...prank?"

The key stopped twirling, and his dark eyebrows jumped toward his bald pate. "A prank? I hope not. I think it may have been a mistake or the alarm got tripped somehow. The fire department is having a look today."

"I suppose you wouldn't bother to check camera footage to see who pulled the alarm." She held her breath, trying to crack a smile.

He shrugged. "That wouldn't do us much good, anyway. Some alarms are out of the camera view. It's not worth investigating."

For you, maybe.

"I hope it's the last one. It interrupted my work." She held up the keychain with her new silver key dangling from it. "Thanks again for the key."

"Yes, ma'am."

She gave him a broad smile before going upstairs. Ugh, he'd called her *ma'am*. He must think her an uptight witch, and she was still none the wiser about who pulled that alarm yesterday to gain access to her so-called office.

When she got back to the conference room, she closed the door behind her and parked herself in front of her laptop. She supposed she could log in to the FBI database and print those two files out again, sending them to a printer in this office, but there would be a trail, and she didn't want to push her luck.

She might not get the opportunity, anyway. If someone at this lab stole those files to get her pulled from this audit, she'd probably hear about it soon enough. And then she'd have to come clean to Jefferson, and even his supervisor, that she was Nat Cooper and investigating a cold case that had involved her.

She worked under a cloud of apprehension for another hour before shooting off an email to Nicole Meloan in the evidence room. It was time to take possession of the case files. Most of these cases were cold, but not all. She wasn't here to solve old cases…except her own. She was here to comb through evidence that had been mishandled over the years, mishandled to the point that it had come to the FBI's attention.

A few seconds after she hit Send on that email, the conference room phone rang. "Natalie Brunetti."

"Hi, Natalie. This is Nicole. Just thought it would be easier to call then send emails back and forth. I believe we have all the case files here that the FBI ordered a few months ago for your audit. If you're missing anything, let me know. I'll contact the King County Sheriff's Department, as they handled all those cases and sent over the material."

"You're an angel. I'll be right down. Do I need a dolly?"

"Everything's already loaded for you on a dolly. You don't even need to come down to fetch it. Jacob, our part-time facilities guy, is here, so I'll have him deliver the boxes to the conference room."

Natalie had already jumped up from her chair in anticipation of collecting the files. At Nicole's words, she dropped back into her seat, disappointment washing over her. She'd wanted to get those files herself. She'd wanted to take a look at the evidence room.

She took a deep breath. She still had the right and the obligation to inspect the evidence-receiving room. "That's perfect. Thank you so much, Nicole. I suppose I can arrange a look at the evidence room another time."

Silence.

"Of course. Give me a heads-up, and I'll show you around."

"I'll give you a heads-up, but I'd rather have a look on my own. I'll be doing the same in all the labs, and I apologize in advance for the intrusion, but that's kind of what an audit is all about."

"I know that. Don't worry about it. Just let me know when you're ready for your inspection."

"Thanks, Nicole." *Another pissed-off customer.*

If she couldn't go down to the evidence room to grab the files herself, she could at least help

Jacob unload. She opened the conference-room door and kicked the doorstop into place.

Five minutes later, a young man with long, dirty blond hair came out of the elevator pushing a dolly stacked with boxes in front of him. Natalie almost salivated at the sight of the boxes. This is what she did, or had been doing for the past few years—inspecting case evidence, looking for anomalies, contradictions, gaps.

By the time Jacob reached the conference room, Natalie was rubbing her hands together. "You must be Jacob. I'm Natalie."

He gave her a shy grin and pointed to the open door. "In here?"

"Yes, please." She swept a hand along one wall. "I made some room here."

Jacob parked the dolly and hoisted the first box from the top of the stack, making it look easy, but she knew how heavy those boxes could be. "Do you want them in any particular order?"

Rapping on the second box with her knuckles, she said, "By case number. See the number in the upper-right corner of the box? Try to match those up. That'll order them by date, too."

"Should be easy. That's how Ms. Meloan had me load them. She's kinda particular."

Natalie released a sigh. She couldn't imagine anything going awry under Nicole's watchful eye…or Michael's, for that matter. This lab had put its troubles behind it when Michael took over, although Dr. Butler seemed to have some doubts.

"It's a good thing she is kinda particular. Makes our job easier." She reached for the next box.

"No, no. Leave it." Jacob settled the first box on the floor and walked back to the dolly. "I'll get all of them. Some are pretty heavy, and you don't know which ones until you try to lift them."

"Okay, I'll do the directing."

As Jacob lifted each box, she checked the case number on the side and pointed to a spot on the floor. The kid didn't even break a sweat.

When he finished, he rested his arm on the dolly's handle. "Better you than me."

"I know." She placed her hands on her hips and surveyed the stack of boxes. "Looks like a lot of work."

"Yeah, it's not just that." He scratched the blond stubble on his chin. "It's what's in those boxes—pictures and stuff with blood on it. Yeah, no thanks."

Tilting her head, she said, "You *are* working in a forensics lab. You'll have to get used to it if you're going to pursue a career in forensic science."

"Me?" He thumped his skinny chest. "I'm no

science major. I'm majoring in journalism. I'll write about these cases, not investigate them."

"If you're on a crime beat, the blood and gore may be unavoidable."

"I plan to avoid crime. Politics, a different kind of blood and gore."

Natalie perched on the edge of the table. "So this is just a part-time job for you, not an internship."

"Yeah, my dad got me the job. He's a deputy with King County." He pointed at the boxes. "You'll probably see his name in there a few times—Reynolds."

Natalie's stomach dropped. Reynolds was the name of one of the cops that worked on Katie's case. In fact, Reynolds interviewed her when she'd reported what happened in the woods. She nodded. "I'll keep an eye out for it. Thanks, Jacob."

She held the door as he wheeled the dolly back into the hallway, and then closed it behind him with a decisive click. It was bound to happen. Marysville was a small town. People might know her. They wouldn't know her married name, Brunetti, but there were probably a few of her high-school classmates that might remember her. She twirled a curl around her finger. Maybe she should wear her hair straightened, and dye it blond, although she doubted Deputy

Reynolds would recognize her. Maybe nobody would. She'd been a Goth girl with heavy, black eyeliner, burgundy lipstick, wearing all black and chunky Doc Martens. Her parents saved her from dying her hair black at the time by refusing to allow it.

Huffing out a breath, she snapped on a pair of gloves and grabbed a notepad and a pen. Crouching in front of the first box, she tipped off the lid. She lifted several items from the box and spread them out on the conference-room table. Then she pulled up a chair and got to work.

In this first case, the cops had found the murder weapon, a knife, but something had gone wrong during the chain of custody and any fingerprints from the knife had become inaccessible and unreadable. Understanding where the chain of custody had broken down posed difficulties. There were failures at many levels.

She took notes on the case and created a file for fingerprints. If all the cases featured print errors, this might go faster, but she had a feeling the cops would've picked up on that immediately.

The next case she grabbed was one of the closed cases, but only because the Creekside Killer, a notorious serial killer in the area, had confessed to it. The investigation still contained anomalies in the finger printing.

So many law-enforcement agencies had lined up to speak to Avery Plank, the Creekside Killer, hopeful they could close out some of their cold cases with a confession from him. Plank did not disappoint. Unfortunately for those cops, a psychopathic serial killer couldn't be trusted. Who knew?

Plank had confessed to one homicide near Kitsap College, and as it had turned out, he was lying. The real killer was only too happy to have Plank take the credit for his crime. There could be more of those right here.

Natalie gave an involuntary shiver. Had the Creekside Killer been stalking her and Katie that night? They'd already been scaring themselves silly in the woods with witchcraft rituals designed to speak to the dead. Turned out they had more to fear from the living than the dead.

The next box contained some bagged evidence—probably the bloody clothes Jacob Reynolds had mentioned earlier. She opened the paper bag carefully and pinched a plastic bag between two fingers, pulling it out. It swung from her fingers as she held it up to the light.

A woman's top, but no blood. It must've contained DNA or hair on it. She dropped the plastic bag onto the table and reached into the other one again. She felt like a kid reaching into a candy jar for a treat, except that the treats were ghastly reminders of long-ago murders.

Natalie plucked up another plastic baggie, a smaller one, and cupped it in her hand. The shiny object inside caught the overhead light and she gasped.

She recognized the necklace…because it was hers.

Chapter Seven

Michael knocked on the conference-room door. After a few seconds of silence, he peered through the slats of the blinds pulled down over the window. He expected to see Natalie on the phone or hunched over her computer. Instead, she was staring at an object in her hand, her mouth slightly agape.

He tapped on the window, and she jerked her head up, her eyes round in her pale face. "C-come in. It's open."

Poking his head in the door, he said, "I hope I'm not disturbing you. I'm heading out for lunch and wanted to invite you to make up for sending you out on your own for dinner last night."

"I could use a break." As she dropped a plastic bag into an evidence bag, she tipped her head toward the boxes lining one wall. "Got started on the deep dive today."

His glance swept the desk in front of her. The paper evidence bag sat on one side of her laptop and a grubby box sat on the other side, its lid on the floor.

She folded down the top of the evidence bag and dropped it into the box. Bending over, she swept up the lid and secured it on the box. Then she jumped to her feet, and began peeling off her blue gloves. "In fact, I'm starving. Same place as yesterday?"

"If you like, but there's a Thai place you should try before you leave." His gaze darted toward the box containing that paper evidence bag. What had she been looking at, and why had she been so anxious to put it away before he entered the room? Maybe she'd just found some incriminating evidence that implicated the lab and everyone in it.

While she fussed with her coat and purse, he cocked his head to the side and memorized the case number and name—Conchas. No regulation that said the investigated couldn't investigate the investigator.

She spun around, her stylish raincoat hanging over one arm, and her expensive leather purse strapped across her body. "Walking or driving?"

"This one's a drive but not too far."

They stepped out of the conference room, and she turned to lock it up with a silver key hanging from a keychain. She tucked the keychain in a side pocket of her purse and patted it. "Got the key from Sam this morning."

"That's a good idea, especially since you now have the case files and boxes from the sheriff's department in here."

"I was going to pick them up, but Nicole had already arranged for Jacob to deliver them to my office, and they were all in order by date already. I never did get a look at the evidence-receiving room, though."

"Nicole is organized. I'm sure she'd be happy to give you a tour of evidence receiving anytime you like."

"Yeah, that's the thing." They stopped in the lobby, where Natalie hung her coat around her shoulders. "She offered, but I told her I didn't want a tour. I'd like to go through the evidence room on my own. I'll be recording my visit, too. I may have ruffled Nicole's feathers."

"Don't worry about it." He held the front door open for her. "She'll get over it. They all will."

"Are you trying to tell me everyone is not as gung ho about this audit as they're pretending to be?"

"Think about it. Someone comes into your place of work where you spend countless hours trying to get it right, and that person pokes into everything and tries to prove you've been doing it all wrong."

"Except it's not you, is it? Your predecessors made the mistakes. The FBI is just trying to find out how it happened so that it doesn't happen again here or at any lab."

"We know that, but it doesn't stop anyone from feeling accused and maybe unsettled." When they reached his car, he opened the door for her and went around to the driver's side.

When he slid behind the wheel, she said, "I hope I'm not making anyone feel that way."

"It's not you. It's the situation. You've impressed everyone, so if Nicole has a problem, let me know."

"She absolutely did not have a problem. Just a little hesitation, which I totally understand."

"Good. Feel free to access any areas of the lab you need." As he started the car and pulled onto the street, Michael glanced at Natalie, who was staring out the window. He hoped that his openness would encourage her to be upfront with him. He'd checked out the online case file for the Katie Fellows disappearance. The case was still open, but the lead detective had put it down as a runaway.

What did the case mean to Natalie today? If it were just a coincidence, she should've mentioned that she'd gone to high school in the area and had been with a friend when that friend had gone missing. Why the secrecy?

The FBI conducts a background investigation when hiring agents, so surely, this must've come up in her past. Of course, departments didn't look at a background every time they gave an assignment, so the Bureau probably hadn't realized her connection to this area when they gave her the gig…and she hadn't told them.

He pointed to the restaurant's red-and-gold awning as he rolled past, looking for a parking spot on the street. "That's it."

Once settled at the table, menus in hand, water in front of them, Michael asked, "Did you get a lot of work done this morning? It looked like you were engrossed when I peeked in the window."

"Engrossed?" She took a gulp of her water. "Yeah, there's a lot to cover. Going over fingerprint mishaps now."

The waitress saved Natalie from any more of Michael's questions, but he had no intention of giving up on this. If she wouldn't tell him what had her so spooked about that file, he'd needle her until she did. Didn't he have a right to know who was going through his lab with a fine-tooth comb and why?

Michael took a sip of his spicy Thai iced tea and stirred the ice with his straw, clinking it against the glass. "I saw you had the Conchas file. Cold case murder of a young woman about fifteen years ago, right?"

"Thirteen. It was thirteen years ago." She picked up her glass quickly, and some of her drink sloshed over the rim, creating a puddle on the table. She dabbed it with a napkin.

"I guess law enforcement couldn't get Avery Plank to confess to that one." He caught a bead of moisture trailing down the side of his glass. "Although I'm sure they tried."

"Plank turned out to be a boon to departments with unsolved murders everywhere, didn't he?" Natalie planted her elbows on the table. "Do you think he was toying with law enforcement by confessing to crimes he didn't commit and leaving them to wonder about crimes he *did* commit?"

Like Katie Fellows?

"Instead of trying to take credit for everything, he was messing with their heads and playing coy about murders he was responsible for." He rubbed his knuckles across his chin. "I wouldn't put it past him. He likes to play games. In the end, detectives have to look at the proof and not just take his word for it. They got burned before with that cold case out at Kitsap College."

"Terrible, how that turned out." Natalie moved her water and tea glasses out of the way, as the waitress delivered their plates of spicy basil fried rice.

"Does the Conchas case have fingerprint issues."

She glanced up from her plate. "I—I really didn't get a chance to delve into the case, yet. After lunch."

Michael gave up for now, and changed the subject to why she chose the FBI and how she liked it so far, although he was sure her choice of career had something to do with what she experienced as a teen. She managed to skirt her motivation for joining the Bureau with trite statements about looking for justice and doing the right thing. Who didn't want those things? Not everyone went in for law enforcement.

As they finished up their lunch, Nicole came sailing into the restaurant and waved when she saw them.

Michael murmured under his breath, "Here's your chance to set Nicole straight on when you're going to invade her space."

Natalie tossed her napkin at him and waved back at Nicole.

Nicole made a detour to their table on her way to the counter. "Work lunch?"

"Always. If I'd known you were coming here, I would've invited you along." Then he wouldn't have had the chance to grill Natalie about the Conchas case—not that he'd gotten anything useful from her.

"Last-minute decision." She waved a piece of paper in the air. "I took a lunch order at the office. Not everyone can afford the luxury of a sit-down lunch outside the office."

"Ouch." Michael clapped a hand over his heart.

"I'm joking. You deserve a break, boss. You know, he's had a rough six months." Nicole patted his shoulder. "But you shouldn't be the only one tasked with making sure our visitor is wined and dined. Natalie, I'd like to invite you to my house for dinner tonight—nothing special, probably takeout and a bottle of wine."

"I don't want to put you out, Nicole. I really don't need wining and dining. I think Michael felt guilty last night, but you all are going to get sick of me at work. You don't need to see me in your homes, too, intruding on your family time."

Nicole's eyes shimmered as she held up one hand. "Well, I live alone, so I'd welcome the company. We don't even have to talk shop."

"If you're certain. I'd love to come over." She pushed away her almost-empty plate. "Just no Chinese."

"I'll surprise you, unless there's something you can't stand." Nicole pressed her fingers to her lips.

"Surprise me." Natalie plucked the check from the edge of the table. "And you're right about it being a luxury to eat out. I need to get back to work."

"We all do." Michael made a grab for the check, but Natalie snatched it away.

"If the staff is going to be inviting me home for dinner, the FBI can cover a few lunches."

They left Nicole waiting for her take-out order, and Michael drove back to the lab. As they parted at the stairs, Natalie turned toward him. "I think Nicole invited me to make up for her hesitancy when I told her I needed to have a look at the evidence-receiving room."

"I think you just caught her off guard earlier. She's not much of a cook, though, so I don't know that you're getting such a good deal."

"You're a terrible boss." She flicked her hair and sauntered back to her office.

She didn't know the half of it.

As soon as he pulled up the chair to his desk and logged in to his computer, he did a search for the Conchas case. He skimmed through the awful details.

Sierra Conchas was a young woman, barely twenty years old, who disappeared on her way home from her part-time job at a gas station's convenience store. Cops discovered her broken-down vehicle on the road that followed the woods. Signs of a scuffle outside the car but no other tire tracks in the vicinity.

Hikers found the body in a ravine days later, partially clothed, bloody, a torn T-shirt beside her. Stab wounds. Michael brought up photos of the crime-scene evidence, which had been processed through this lab at the time.

No knife was found. No DNA. Fiber from a black beanie or maybe a ski mask, but no DNA on that, either. The blood on Sierra's shirt belonged to her. No rape, so no bodily fluids left behind. Torn fingernails, as if she put up a fight, but no skin cells beneath the nails.

Damn. Not much to go on here. Also, not the MO of the Creekside Killer, who usually strangled his victims and left them beside water. But what had Natalie found so interesting about this case? It didn't mimic Katie's case in any way, except for the setting. And to face facts, in the Pacific Northwest, most murder victims were dumped in the forests, down ravines, off trails, in the water.

He clicked through the pictures on his computer and stopped at a baggie containing jewelry, or at least a silver pendant shaped in a circle with four knots through it.

He skipped back and forth through the file to discover that the pendant was around Sierra's neck, but Sierra's mother had never seen it before. He checked the date of Sierra's death against the date of Katie's disappearance. Sierra had been murdered about seven months after Katie disappeared.

Could the pendant have belonged to Katie?

Had her parents reported any jewelry along with the clothing she was wearing when she went missing? Maybe Natalie thought the two cases were linked?

He jumped when his phone rang. He'd become as absorbed in the case as Natalie had been.

When he glanced as his display, knots tightened in his gut. A call from Detective Ibarra, the detective investigating his wife's murder, usually brought bad news.

He closed his eyes as he answered. "Wilder here."

"Michael, it's Gil Ibarra. I know you probably don't want to hear from me."

"That's not true, Vince. I want to hear from you when you call to tell me you've found the person who killed Raine. Is that what you're calling about?"

"Afraid not, Michael." Ibarra took a breath, and Michael's shoulders tensed. "Full toxicology report finally came back on Raine's autopsy."

"Thought you had that already."

"Preliminary toxicology. She had a lot of substances in her system."

"I'm aware." Michael's hand gripped the arm of his chair. "What did you find this time around?"

"You said your wife, er, Raine had been on antidepressants, and we found a bottle of Lexapro in her purse—ten-milligram pills. Do you know if this was her regular dosage?"

Michael pinched the bridge of his nose. "I'm not sure what she took or how much. She hid that from me, so it wouldn't come up in the custody dispute."

"The medical examiner said the usual dose is ten milligrams, and those are the pills Raine had." Ibarra made a clicking noise with his tongue. "But Raine had a lot more than that in her system, probably five times that amount."

"What are you saying? Raine took an overdose of her meds? You can't be suggesting suicide now, right? She was strangled with some cloth tie, or did you get that wrong, too?" Michael's heart was raging in his chest.

"She was strangled, so not suicide, but if someone was able to ply her with an overdose of meds before taking her out to that trail before killing her, we're not looking at a stranger here. No, Raine's killer knew her. Knew her very well."

Chapter Eight

After studying the pendant more closely, Natalie was convinced it was hers. How did her pendant from that night wind up around Sierra Conchas's neck when she was murdered? The person who killed Katie must be the same person who killed Sierra. This had to be the answer.

She'd given her witch's knot to Katie that night to ward off the evil spirits of the forest, or some such nonsense. Katie had been wearing that pendant when she'd disappeared. It had never been found. Natalie hadn't even thought about it at the time, and Katie's mother wouldn't have reported it as something her daughter was wearing because she didn't know Natalie had given it to Katie.

Natalie's family had moved out of the area before she graduated from high school and before Sierra's murder. Had Sierra's mother told the police that the necklace didn't belong to her daughter. Did the police ever wonder where it had come from?

She knew being close to the scene of Katie's disappearance and looking at other cases would yield clues. This had to be the first of many. Katie's killer had taken her pendant and left it on another victim. Was that part of his MO? Had he taken items from his victims and given them to other victims?

Sierra's killer had stabbed her, but the police never found any blood in the area where Katie went missing. They hadn't found Katie at all. Where had he taken her? What had he done with her?

When they took off running in opposite directions that night, she'd run toward the campsite area, even though it had been empty. But Katie had foolishly barreled toward Devil's Edge itself, toward the steep drop-off into the craggy rocks. The sheriff's department had searched the rocks, though. They hadn't found anything.

Natalie thought she'd heard a car's engine that night. Had their pursuer somehow gotten Katie in his car and taken her away? Her breathing became shallow, and her fingertips started going numb.

She made her mind a blank and took deep breaths through her nose from her stomach until they filled her chest, and then released them slowly through her mouth. She'd never taken meds for her anxiety, but a behavioral therapist had taught her to control the onset of a panic attack through modulated breathing. It worked most of the time.

Water helped, too. She pushed away from the desk and locked the conference room door behind her. A lot of good that lock had done her this morning with Michael spying on her through the blinds, but she'd look even more suspicious if she closed those blinds and tried to keep everyone out. She decided to stop at his office on the way down to the breakroom just to keep the lines of communication open.

She slowed down when she approached his closed office door. He usually left his door wide open for his staff. She tapped on it.

He answered in a muffled voice. "Come in."

She eased open the door, and he turned from where he was standing at the window, hands in his pockets. His stormy scowl softened a tad when he saw her.

"Do you need something?"

She didn't, but he obviously did. She stepped into his office and shut the door behind her. "Are you okay?"

"Yeah. What do you mean?" He tried a smile, but it didn't work.

She placed a hand flat on her belly. "It's not your daughter. Is Ivy alright?"

"Ivy's fine." He ran a hand through his black

hair. "I guess it's no use pretending to an FBI agent. Have a seat."

She perched on the edge of a chair facing his desk, as he took his own advice and dropped to his swivel chair.

"I just had some interesting news about my wife's murder." He swiped a hand across his mouth. "They found elevated levels of her anti-depressant medication in her system."

"What does that mean? Not suicide?"

"No, she was definitely strangled with a gar-rote, but the detective is implying that some-one drugged her first. Someone she knew. How could a stranger be able to slip her meds?"

Natalie bit her bottom lip. "What about at a bar? Had she been drinking at a bar? Someone could've slipped her something and then fol-lowed her to the woods."

He folded his hands in front of him, his knuck-les white. "The day Raine died she'd been at my house to visit Ivy. The babysitter, Natasha, had been home at the time. When Raine left my house, she took our dog for a walk. Natasha wasn't sure, so she called me at work, and I told her it was fine. Raine never returned."

"And the dog?" Natalie tucked her hands be-neath her thighs as her knees bounced up and down.

"Peaches never returned. Never found her

leash. The point is—" he flattened his hands on his desk, his thumbs touching "—Raine didn't go anywhere else. She took the dog out for a walk and ended up dead on Devil's Edge Trail. I always figured this was a crime of opportunity. She'd gone to the trail for a walk, someone with bad intentions saw her and killed her. Now…"

"Now it looks like someone drugged her first." She scooted her chair closer to his desk and leaned forward. "Maybe Raine took the meds herself. Maybe she did plan to kill herself."

"And someone finished the job for her? Far-fetched."

She drummed her fingers on his desk. "She could've had a pact with someone. What if she wanted to die, anyway, and figured she'd stick it to you on her way out by having someone kill her to pin the blame on you."

"Whoa." He held up his hands and crossed one finger over the other. "Raine had issues, but even she wouldn't go that far. You've got quite the imagination."

"It's happened before, hasn't it? I've seen a few cases where people didn't want their families to lose out on their life-insurance money with a suicide, so they staged a murder." She swallowed. "Why did the cops zero in on you at first? Was it just because you were the husband, and the two of you were in a custody dispute?"

"That and I didn't have a clear alibi. After Natasha told me Raine had taken Peaches for a walk, I didn't feel like running into Raine when I got home. So, I left work a little early and drove to the woods to take a walk." He spread his hands. "Cell-phone service is spotty on some of those trails and the cops couldn't track my phone continuously."

"Definitely a problem." She twirled a finger in the air. "Does this new information put you back on their radar?"

"It doesn't help, but a witness saw me coming out of the woods and getting into my car at about the same time as Raine's murder. Saved me."

"Thank God for that. I guess Peaches couldn't do much to protect Raine?"

He put his hands about eighteen inches apart. "She was...is a little pug."

The knock on the door startled Natalie, and she pulled back from Michael's desk. His tale had her spellbound.

He leaned back in his chair. "Come in."

Nicole popped her head inside the office. "Oh, good, both of you. I have the food all ordered for delivery, Natalie. Seven o'clock? I'll email you my address."

"Seven is fine, Nicole. Thanks."

Nicole nodded her curly head. "And, Michael, is it okay if I take off a little early today? I don't have any more deliveries scheduled, and I have a few errands to run."

"I hope not on my account." Natalie stood and smoothed her slacks.

"That's all taken care of. I have a few personal matters."

"Sure, no problem." Michael stood and stretched, and Natalie had the satisfaction of noticing that the storm clouds had cleared from his brow.

Nicole remained in the doorway, so Natalie scooted past her. "I'll look out for your email, Nicole. Thanks, again."

For the rest of the afternoon, Raine's homicide occupied Natalie's thoughts, replacing the mystery of how the pendant got around Sierra's neck.

Michael had been through the ringer these past six months. She'd remembered how the cops had suspected Katie's boyfriend, Zane, in her disappearance, and it had wreaked havoc on his life. He had to transfer schools—just like she'd moved away.

She couldn't imagine what Michael had been through, trying to take care of his daughter while law enforcement had him as their prime suspect in his wife's murder.

By the time she wrapped up her work, quiet had settled on the second floor of the lab, and she had an hour to go back to her hotel, change, pick up a bottle of wine and make it to Nicole's place.

She glanced down the hallway toward Michael's office, the door firmly closed. He hadn't stopped by on his way out to say good night. Had their discussion this afternoon unsettled him?

When she'd seen him in distress at his window, she couldn't help herself. Something about a strong man showing his vulnerable side plucked all her strings. Her ex-husband had never shown her that side. Joe didn't have any demons at all, and at first, she thought that's what she needed in a partner. She'd had enough for the two of them, and Joe just couldn't handle her tormented side.

She didn't blame him. They'd parted as friends. But she didn't want a friend as a spouse. She wanted someone who understood her down to the core. Someone with his own darkness to wrestle. Michael had that darkness.

Snorting, she locked her office door. She'd just met a potential wife killer, and she had him pegged as her next spouse.

An hour later, bottle of pinot noir on the seat beside her, Natalie followed her GPS to Nicole's house. She did a double take when she passed the turnoff to the campsite near the Devil's Edge Trail.

The location of Nicole's home defied Natalie's expectations of a modern condo in the heart of the city. Older homes tended to hug the forest line, unless some developer had come in to rip down an outdated house and put up an expensive cabin with glass walls and wooden decks with hot tubs.

As she pulled in front of Nicole's house, she saw immediately that no fancy developer had touched this place. Nicole had definitely made some improvements to the original, though. A neat, wooden fence ringed the property. Tidy flower boxes adorned the windows, and fall blooms added a touch of color to the freshly painted clapboard front. Beige pavers with flecks of gold created a path to the front door beneath the towering pines. Even the trees had been trimmed into manageable accents to the house without overpowering it.

Nicole opened the door before Natalie had a chance to knock. "Welcome. I'm glad you found me out here."

"What a lovely spot." Natalie held up the bottle of wine. "Hope you like red."

"Perfect." Nicole studied the label. "It'll go with the Indian food I ordered. I hope you like Indian. I didn't get anything too spicy."

"The spicier the better."

Crooking her finger, Nicole said, "Follow me to the kitchen. You can pour while I plate the food. The delivery guy just left."

Natalie squeezed into the tiny kitchen behind Nicole. Her host apparently hadn't had the time, inclination or money to spruce up the inside of her place as much as the outside. The old-fashioned kitchen sported the original linoleum in a faded gold, with the dated appliances lined up against both walls.

At least the food smelled good. The pungent aroma of curry hung in the air, with an undercurrent of warm, sweet cardamom, which gave the kitchen a homey feel.

Nicole reached into a cupboard and took out two wineglasses. "Fill 'em up."

As Nicole dumped the food from the cartons into glass serving dishes, Natalie filled each small wineglass almost to the halfway point. She had to drive back to her hotel, and she and her rental car were still getting acquainted.

"Should I put the raita in a dish?" Nicole held up a small Styrofoam cup of the yogurt accompaniment to their spicy food.

"Nah. Let's live dangerously and spoon it out from the take-out container. In fact, we could've done that with all the food and saved you some dishes."

Nicole shook her head. "It's bad enough that I can't cook. I can at least present someone else's food in a pleasing way."

They carried the dishes to the table, where Nicole had set two places with World Market-type colorful plates and placemats. They sat across from each other and toasted.

As they clinked glasses, Nicole said, "To a speedy and satisfactory audit."

"I will definitely drink to that—and to one that doesn't ruffle anyone's feathers."

"About that—" Nicole gave her a glance from the corner of her eye "—you just took me by surprise today when you suggested you wanted a look at the evidence-receiving room on your own. It's my little fiefdom, and I'm protective over it. Of course, I understand why you need to survey it, just like you will for any other area of the lab."

"And I understand your balking at the idea. I'd be the same if someone wanted to look over my files."

Nicole raised her glass again. "So here's to understanding all around."

As they ate and chatted about the lab, Natalie's gaze wandered over Nicole's shoulder to take in the pictures on the sideboard. She zeroed in on one with Nicole in a wedding dress, standing next to a smiling man in a tux. She had to hand it to Nicole. Natalie didn't have any of her ex on display, wedding or otherwise.

Nicole twisted her head around. "Ah, my wedding picture."

"Sorry. Didn't mean to be nosy." Natalie ripped

off a corner from the naan on her plate. "I'm divorced, too, but I boxed up my wedding photos."

Nicole swirled her wine before taking a sip. "I'm not divorced. I'm a widow."

Natalie put down her fork and reached across the table to squeeze Nicole's hand. "I'm so sorry. What happened?"

"Suicide."

Natalie squeezed harder. "That's awful, Nicole."

Nicole sniffed and dabbed her nose with a napkin. "He was a cop. Had a lot of those typical cop problems."

Feeling as if she'd been intrusive enough for one night, Natalie went back to her food and waited for Nicole to continue…if she wanted.

She didn't.

"Anyway, do you like the food? I love Indian, and we have just two restaurants in town. This is the better one. The other is more for quick takeout."

"It's delicious. Great choice."

After that bombshell, conversation lagged between the two of them. Questions swarmed in Natalie's head, but Nicole had shut down any more discussion about her deceased husband.

She helped Nicole in the kitchen and when they finished, Nicole offered her coffee and homemade cookies.

"It's funny. I don't like to cook, but I do like to bake, and I think I'm pretty good at it."

"I'm sure you are, but honestly, I can't eat another bite of food. Maybe you should bring the cookies to the lab tomorrow and put them out in the lunchroom."

"I've done that before." Nicole placed two plastic containers in a bag and pushed it toward Natalie. "If you're not going to have a cookie, take some of this leftover food. You can bring it for lunch tomorrow…unless you and Michael are going to make your lunch dates a habit."

Natalie glanced sharply at Nicole, but she'd ducked into the fridge to put away more food.

Is that what the lab thought? She and Michael were on lunch dates while the rest of them worried about what she'd find in the audit that might implicate them in wrongdoing?

She picked up the bag. "That is a good idea. Then I can use more of my per diem for dinner instead of spending it on *work* lunches."

Nicole held up the bottle of wine. "You're going to leave this with me to finish off, aren't you?"

"Better you than me. I gotta drive home." Natalie made a move toward the door. "Thanks again, Nicole. Dinner was great, but I hope everyone is not taking Michael seriously and inviting the orphan home for dinner."

"They probably will." Nicole winked. "We all want to stay on your good side."

"This doesn't hurt." Natalie raised the plastic bag of food and swung it in the air with her fingertips.

Nicole walked her out to her car, and Natalie lifted her face to the mist that had rolled in and clung to the needles of the pines. "Smells good out here."

"It's lovely. That's why I won't move."

"Don't blame you." Why should Nicole move? Had this been her husband's house? Had he ended his life here?

Natalie climbed into the car and placed the bag of food on the passenger side. "Thanks again."

She reversed out of Nicole's driveway and bumped along the access road back to the highway. Her fingers scrabbled around the steering wheel and column to find the high beams. She didn't want to hit any unsuspecting animals crossing the road. She worried less about people and cars, as not too many populated the highway or forest at this time of night—not typically.

When she hit the first curve in the road, she had to pump the brakes. She should be used to hopping into rental cars and adapting given the amount of traveling she did for the Bureau, but every car seemed different.

A red light blinked on the dashboard, and she

dropped her gaze to read it. Some weird-shaped icon blinked back at her. How the hell was she supposed to read that? Couldn't be the gas. The rental company had given her a car with a full tank, and she'd hardly driven anywhere since she arrived in Marysville.

The road dipped and the car picked up speed. At least it was still running. She tapped the brakes, and the car seemed to whoosh forward. At the bottom of the incline, the road snaked to the right. Heading into the turn faster than she wanted, Natalie eased on the brakes. The sponginess of the pressure made her press harder. The car shuddered but didn't slow down.

She gripped the steering wheel and turned it slightly to navigate the turn, while pressing the brake pedal. She made the turn okay, but the brakes were not responding to her pressure.

Another incline and the car went faster. She didn't want to stomp on the brakes and put the car into a tailspin. She tried tapping, but all she got for her efforts was a clunking sound from the engine.

As she came out of the descent, another curve awaited her. This time she applied full pressure to the brakes, but her foot almost when through the floorboard. As she fumbled for the button for the emergency brake, an animal darted into the road, its gleaming eyes pinned to the oncoming car.

With the brake pedal on the floor and one of her knuckles jabbing the emergency brake, she jerked the wheel to avoid the animal, and the car lurched once and then started zooming down a hill, straight for a tree.

Chapter Nine

Michael kicked a tree stump with the toe of his hiking boot. He'd promised himself not to come out to this spot again. What good did it do? There were no answers among the trees. No clues left on the trail.

If the cops got wind of his nighttime sojourns out here, he'd probably make it back to the top of their suspect list. The news from Detective Ibarra today had tilted him off course, had crushed his theory about a stranger homicide.

Raine had been hanging out with some shady characters, but murder? The cops had already checked out her boyfriend, and he'd had a better alibi than Michael.

Maybe Natalie had been right. Maybe Nicole took additional pills on her own. She'd had no self-restraint. She could've reasoned the more pills the better. Some stranger had taken advantage of her disorientation and killed her. There had been no sexual assault, but her clothes had been ripped. She could've fought off her attacker's sexual battery, and he'd struck back and killed her.

He tipped back his head and yelled to the night sky, "Enough!"

As he turned to leave, a sickening thud echoed through the forest. That was no animal, unless some critter had recently acquired a metal coat.

He jogged down the path, back to his car, which was parked just off the road. He got in and turned on his headlights, then eased forward, sweeping the empty highway. Looking in his rearview mirror, he saw smoke rising from the forest on the other side of the road.

He threw his car in Reverse and backed up several feet. Then he pulled it off the road and jumped out. His nostrils twitched at the smell of burning rubber. As he got closer to the smoke, his flashlight picked out skid marks on the road leading into the forest.

He ran into the underbrush, where a car had just forged a new trail. He followed the broken branches and flattened bushes into the woods, and his adrenaline ramped up even more when he spotted a car, its front end crumped against a tree.

Smoke continued to pour from the damaged vehicle, and the smell of gasoline permeated the air. He scrambled toward the car and peered through the driver's-side window.

His heart slammed against his chest as Natalie pushed against the airbag, which was pinning her to the seat. He tried the door handle, but the lock was engaged, so he pounded on the window.

Natalie turned her pale face toward him, and several seconds later, he heard the locks click. He yanked open the door and pulled her out of the car and away from the airbag.

He shouted, even though she was right next to him. "We need to get away from the car. I smell gasoline."

"My purse." She reached around him.

"I'll get it. Move." He ducked into the car and grabbed her purse and a plastic bag from the floor of the front seat.

He stumbled back and joined her several feet away. "Let's keep moving toward the road and call nine-one-one. Are you alright? Can you walk?"

"I'm okay." She dabbed her fingers against an abrasion on her forehead.

When she swayed on her feet, he swept her up in his arms and carried her back toward the highway. As he tromped down the trail her car had blazed through earlier, her head fell on his shoulder, the curly tendrils of her hair tickling his chin. The ease with which she fit into his arms, and against his chest, didn't surprise him. He knew, from at least this afternoon, when she'd sensed his turmoil, that wrapping his arms around her would feel right.

A crackling noise behind them spurred on Michael's footsteps, and he didn't put Natalie down until he reached the asphalt.

Clinging to his shirt, she craned her head around. "The car's on fire. Oh, my God. You saved my life. I couldn't get out from under that airbag. I thought those things were supposed to protect you."

"I think you were just panicked. You would've eventually shimmied out from under it." He slipped his phone from the pocket of his jeans and tapped it for 911.

"Don't downplay your heroism. If you hadn't come along when you did, I'd probably still be stuck in that car, which is now burning." She tilted her head back and sniffed the smoky air.

Michael spoke into the phone to the 911 operator, asking for an ambulance.

When he hung up, Natalie said, "I don't need an ambulance. I'm okay." She examined her forearms. "I think I'm going to have some bruises from the airbag, but I never lost consciousness, and I'm not injured anywhere."

"Never hurts to get checked out, and you should be grateful the airbag went off, or you might have gone through the windshield into that tree. What the hell happened, anyway? I assume you were coming home from Nicole's place."

"I was." Hugging her purse to her chest, she said, "The brakes on the car went out. It was kind of a perfect storm. I was coming out of an incline and a curve, and an animal ran into the road. I swerved to avoid it and crashed through the tree line. Luckily, I met bushes and underbrush first before running into the first tree. I think the car was slowing down by the time I hit the tree."

"Brake failure? On a new rental car?"

"I'm no mechanic." She held up her arms, which were already turning blue with bruising. "But I pressed on the brake pedal, eased it on and finally stomped on it. At first it was spongy; then my foot went right to the floor. Maybe it's a good thing I saw that animal and pulled off in a relatively safe area. It's almost as if…"

"As if what?" He plucked a leaf from her hair, his fingers lingering over a soft curl.

"This place, this area." She bit her bottom lip. "It's where…"

"It's near Devil's Edge." Where Raine was murdered and where Natalie's friend had disappeared. Did she think the animal was infused with Katie's spirit and had saved her?

He opened his mouth, but an approaching siren saved him from spilling the beans and admitting he'd spied on her. Too bad she couldn't trust him enough to tell him. He'd trusted her, and it had been a while since he felt he could trust a woman.

"Is that why you were nearby?" She placed a hand on his arm. "You went back?"

"I did, but I'm done with it. I'll let the sheriff's department do its job and find the answers that are evading me."

"I'm glad you did go back. If you hadn't, I might not be standing here beside you."

He put an arm around her and pulled her close, whispering in her hair. "And that would've been a tragedy."

He didn't get to gauge her response, and maybe she didn't even hear him because the emergency vehicles pulled up, bathing both of them in red lights, assaulting their ears with wailing sirens.

An hour later, the fire department had doused the car fire, and an EMT had checked out Natalie's vitals and injuries. She'd escaped what could've been a disaster pretty much unscathed.

He'd had to explain to the cops that he'd been out for a drive, but nobody seemed to think it odd that his drive had taken him past the exact spot where his wife had been murdered.

Natalie had called the rental-car company to give them the bad news, but they'd been more concerned about the faulty brakes and a possible lawsuit than blaming Natalie. They'd promised her a new car delivered to her hotel first thing in the morning.

As the emergency personnel wrapped up and cleaned up, Michael took Natalie's arm. "You're sure you're okay?"

"Clean bill of health from the EMTs." She dusted her hands together and winced.

"You're gonna have some wicked bruises on your arms and probably your chest from that airbag."

She pressed her fingers against her chest. "Feeling it already."

"I'm driving you back to your hotel. Do you have everything?"

She held up her purse and the plastic bag. "Got my purse and my leftover Indian food from Nicole's dinner."

"You mean I risked my life going back into that car for Indian food?"

She winked. "You obviously have never had the biriyani from Taj Majal."

"I have, actually. It all makes sense now." He yelled over to a deputy. "Are you done with us? I'm taking Natalie to her hotel."

The deputy waved back. "All good."

Michael opened the door for her and had to

help her inside as she stiffly lowered herself to the passenger seat.

When he got behind the wheel, he said, "I hope you have some ibuprofen in your room. You're going to be sore."

"Going to be?" She rubbed the back of her neck. "It's already kicking in."

When they arrived at her hotel, Michael hurried to the passenger side of the car to help her out. He snagged her purse and bag of food from the floor, then wrapped his arm around her waist.

As they walked through the sliding doors of her hotel, she extricated herself from his hold. "Thanks, Michael. I can manage from here."

"No way. I'm not getting on the bad side of the FBI by neglecting one of its agents. I'll see you up to your room and get you settled."

"You don't have to get home?"

"Ivy was sleeping when I left, and my sister was ensconced in her bedroom perusing dating apps on her phone."

Natalie wrinkled her nose. "Brave girl."

She didn't object again when he placed a hand on the small of her back and steered her toward the elevators.

As they rode up to the third floor, he said, "I don't expect to see you at the lab tomorrow. You should rest."

"That's the last thing I need to do. If I lie

down for hours, my body is going to be too stiff to move. The EMT told me to stretch and move around." She tapped her keycard against her door, and it clicked open.

"Don't know how much stretching and moving around you're going to do at the office." He bent over and opened the tiny fridge. "You want the food in here or did your near-death experience make you hungry?"

"You can put it away, but if there's a small bottle of wine in the minibar, I'll take it."

He studied the minibar. "You want something stronger?"

"No, but help yourself."

He plucked a bottle of chardonnay from the fridge and twisted off the cap. "Only the finest. Is there a glass somewhere?"

She bounced on the edge of the bed and held out her hand, wiggling her fingers. "I'll drink it from the bottle."

He handed it to her, and she placed it to her lips and took a long draw from the bottle.

Cupping the bottle between her hands, she said, "That was scary. I've never even been in a fender bender before."

"I'm glad you're okay. Maybe I was meant to be in that spot one last time." He sat in the desk chair and hunched forward, his elbows on his knees. "How was your dinner with Nicole, otherwise?"

"It was good. Food was delicious, and the conversation flowed. She knows a lot about crime." She picked at the label on the bottle. "Nicole told me about her husband. That's awful. Did it happen here or before she moved here?"

"It happened here, just around the time I started at the lab. I'm surprised she told you about it. She usually doesn't talk about her husband's death."

"I'm afraid I asked her. I saw the wedding picture and assumed she was divorced like me. Just used it as a conversation starter, and it had the opposite effect." She took another sip from the bottle. "She said he was a cop. Was it a depression thing?"

"He was a cop. You met Jacob Reynolds, our part-time gofer. His dad, Max Reynolds, was Frank Meloan's partner."

Natalie put a hand to her throat. "Wow, so many connections in this town."

Michael knew exactly what Natalie was thinking, as Max Reynolds had been assigned to Katie Fellows's case. It felt weird having this deception between them. Why wouldn't she just tell him? Did she think he'd report her to the FBI to get her off the audit and out of their hair? She must.

He stood suddenly and stretched. "I'd better

get going. Nobody is going to raise their eyebrows if you don't show up."

"I'll be fine." She scooted off the edge of the bed and put the bottle of wine on the credenza. "If my neck gets any worse, I'll take a trip to urgent care. Otherwise, the rental-car company is delivering another car tomorrow morning, and I'll be there."

"You could sue the company, you know. How do brakes fail on a newish rental car?"

"I suppose they'll have to do some accident investigation first to make sure I wasn't at fault. You know the cops had me blow into a breathalyzer. Good thing I had just one glass of wine at Nicole's and plenty of food."

As she stood in front of him, he could smell the fruity aroma from the chardonnay on her breath. Good thing she hadn't downed a mini bottle before getting in the car.

He placed one hand on her shoulder. "I'm just glad it wasn't more serious for you."

Her eyelashes fluttered, and her lips parted.

Was he going to do this? How could he with secrets between them? He'd had enough deception from Raine throughout their marriage. He'd vowed never to accept that poison again...no matter how tempting the fruit.

Obviously not hampered by the same principles, Natalie decided for him. She stood on her tiptoes and leaned forward to place a gentle kiss on his lips. "Th-that's a thank-you. Or maybe that's the wine."

He'd stood frozen just in case it was the wine, but she kissed him again, pressing her soft lips against his and winding one arm around his neck.

He kissed her back this time but kept his hands to himself, sort of a half-assed compromise between his ethics and his lust.

She drew back, placing her hands on his chest. "Bad idea? I thought, you know, we had something."

"We *could* have something." He shoved his hands in his pockets. "But I already had a relationship built on distrust, and I'm not going there again. It almost cost me my freedom."

Her fingers curled against his chest. "Distrust? Is it because I'm doing an audit of your lab? It's my job, Michael. It's not personal."

"Oh, I think it's very personal, Nat... Nat Cooper."

Chapter Ten

Natalie's hands dropped from Michael's chest, and she took a step back from him and all the promise that had been in his eyes a minute earlier. "What do you know? Does everyone know?"

Folding his arms, he perched on the edge of the desk behind him. "Why don't you just tell me?"

"You know my maiden name, so you must know about my connection to this area." She fell onto the bed and crossed her arms behind her head. "You must know about Katie Fellows...and that I was with her the night she disappeared."

"No thanks to you. I had to sleuth around to find out—not because I wanted dirt on you. I want to know you—the real Natalie." He swung the chair around and straddled it, crossing his arms over the back and resting his chin on them. "Tell me what happened and tell me why you're hiding it."

He wanted to know the real Natalie? If he did, he'd probably run away, like Joe had.

"The why is easy. If the Bureau knew about

my history here, they never would've sent me to look into the lab. I need to look into the lab. I think the muddling of evidence here is the reason Katie's case got short shrift."

"And maybe the fact that her body was never found." He licked his lips. "Is the first part harder to talk about?"

"Not really. I've been over it in my head a million times. I've talked about it and analyzed it from every direction with my therapist." She lifted her head. "Don't."

"Therapy is good. You need it for…trauma?"

"It happened fourteen years ago, when I was a teenager. You'd think I'd be over it by now, but I can't shake the memory of it. Maybe, and I know this sounds bad, but maybe if Katie's body had been found and someone had been tried and convicted of her murder, I could move on."

"Doesn't sound bad. It makes sense. That's why you're here. So you can move on. Maybe you can start that process by telling me what happened that night."

She scooched up to the top of the bed and plumped some pillows against the headboard. Might as well get comfortable. "It was all my fault. I was into Wiccan stuff and all that nonsense. I was the new kid my junior year of high school. I was a Goth girl at a school that didn't have Goth, so Katie glommed on to me from the start. I piqued her curiosity, I guess. Anyway, we kind of formed a clique with another girl, Bella Owens."

"Is she still in town?"

"She's in Seattle, but her family still lives here. They wouldn't be too pleased to see me show up on their doorstep." She drew her knees to her chest and wrapped her arms around her legs. "Bella couldn't make it that night, but Katie and I snuck out to the woods to conjure spirits."

"Let me guess, at midnight?"

"Not quite, but late enough that it was pitch-black. We had our little offering on the floor of the forest, and then we started hearing noises from the trees. Once we figured out the noises were human, not animal, that's when we made a run for it." She leaned her chin on her knees. "I figured she'd run toward the campsite area, like me, but she took off toward the drop-off at the end of Devil's Edge."

Michael asked, "Did you call the police?"

"Not right away. I made my way home and texted Katie the rest of the night, but she never answered. I didn't get a wink of sleep and when Katie's mom called our house that morning to ask if Katie was with me, I went into a panic. I told my parents what happened, and they marched me down to the sheriff's station in town—right into Deputy Reynolds's office."

"Did you see anyone that night? Hear a voice? A smell? Anything?"

"The voice was distorted, just like out of a horror movie. That's what sent us fleeing through the woods. Didn't see or smell anything but woods and pine." She scooped the bedspread in her hands, curling her fingers into the material. "And I didn't tell them the entire truth."

"You left out the Wiccan ritual."

"I didn't want everyone blaming me more than they already did. Katie was a good girl before I showed up. I led her down a dark trail—one that literally got her killed." A tear leaked from the corner of her eye, and she brushed it away.

Michael sprung from his chair and sat on the side of the bed, next to her. He took her hand and rubbed his thumb in a circle on her palm. "You were a dumb kid. You both were. My friends and I could've died a half a dozen times with the stunts we pulled in high school—and that really would've been our faults. But what happened to Katie isn't your fault or hers—just the deviant who snatched her."

"I have to uncover what happened to Katie, Michael. It's the only way I can live with this. There had to have been more and better evidence collected from the woods. The forensic lab's mishandling of that evidence allowed a murder to walk."

"Wait, wait." He lunged for his jacket, which was hanging on the back of a chair, and plunged his hand in the pocket, withdrawing his phone. He swiped across the display. He held out his phone. "Wiccan pendant."

She stared at the picture of her necklace on Michael's phone. "How did you even figure that out?"

"I saw you looking at something in a baggie when I showed up for lunch today, and I noted the case you had spread out before you. Didn't take me long when I researched that case to figure out this was what you were looking at. Is it yours? Is that what freaked you out?"

"It's mine. I gave it to Katie that night when we started hearing sounds from the woods. It was supposed to ward off evil spirits, but I guess I should've given her something to ward off evil humans."

"Your pendant that Katie had when she disappeared ended up around another murder victim's throat. Unless a random killer came across this pendant in the woods, picked it up and decided to use it in his next murder, the person who abducted and probably killed Katie is the same person who killed Sierra Conchas."

"Exactly. And Sierra Conchas *is* one of my assigned cold cases."

Michael got it, and with no judgment aimed

at her. For the first time in a while, Natalie felt a lightness in her chest, the ability to take a full breath and release it. Why had she waited to tell him the truth?

She twirled a lock of hair around her finger. "I guess with all this knowledge, you could torpedo my audit here. But they'd probably just send someone else in my place."

"Is that what you think I'd do?"

"You weren't happy about my arrival." She leveled a finger at him. "Admit it. Lou Gray is not the only one at the lab who resented my presence. He just didn't hide it the way most of you did. If I'd told you all this at the start, you would've had me on the first plane back to DC."

"Maybe. Is that why you—" he slid off the bed and pocketed his phone "—showed some interest in me?"

She stifled a laugh. "I'm not that devious. I showed interest in you because I like the way that one lock of black hair keeps falling into your face. I like the way your blue eyes light up your otherwise scowling complexion when something excites you. I like the way your lips curve up every time you mention your daughter. And I like the way you look at me."

"What way is that?" His eyes smoldered and his nostrils flared.

"Just like that."

He hesitated before stuffing his arms in the sleeves of his jacket. "I'm not going to report you to the FBI. I'm not going to interfere with your investigation into the lab. And I might even be able to help you."

She scrambled off the bed. "Really? You'd do that?"

"I know what it means to have questions, to want justice." He cupped her face with one hand. "And I know what it is to feel guilt, even when everyone tells you it's unwarranted."

"Thank you, Michael. I don't want to get you into any trouble at the lab."

"What trouble? The lab collected and analyzed evidence for some cold cases, and two of them now seem linked through that witch's-knot necklace. Sierra Conchas's case is on your radar, and now the Katie Fellows case is, too."

"But nobody knows about that pendant—nobody but us."

"Maybe we should keep it that way for now." He kissed her swiftly on the lips, as if any longer contact would ignite an inferno, and made a beeline for the door. "If you feel worse tomorrow, go straight to urgent care."

When the door closed behind him, Natalie raised her fingers to her mouth and pressed them against her lips, imprinting his kiss there for the rest of the night ahead.

Who knew being honest had its perks?

She downed the last sip in the little wine bottle and tossed it in the trash. As she turned toward the bathroom to get ready for bed, a knock on the door stopped her.

A rush of warm, stickiness flooded her body. Had Michael changed his mind? She launched herself at the door and pulled it open. "I'm glad you..."

Her words trailed off as she stared at a man in blue scrubs, his blond hair tousled, as if he'd just spent all night in surgery. Her brain fogged over. Had the EMTs sent someone back here to check on her? Had they discovered something off in her vitals?

"Y-yes?"

"It is you. I wasn't sure when I saw you at Thai Boat, but face-to-face, yeah. Nat Cooper."

Natalie stepped back, hiding halfway behind the door, blood roaring in her ears. "I don't know what you're talking about. That's not my name."

"C'mon, Nat." The man clawed through his hair with his fingers, making it stand on end even more. "It's me. Zane. Zane Tolbert."

Natalie clapped a hand over her mouth. Of course, it was Zane. Hair had turned a dirty blond, but he still had a smattering of freckles across his nose, and he hadn't added an ounce of fat on his tall, lanky frame. Katie'd had the biggest crush on Zane, and they'd just started getting exclusive when she disappeared.

She hissed through her fingers. "What are you doing here?"

"I wanted until that guy left, Michael Wilder. Honestly, if he'd spent much more time in here with you alone, I was going to charge in here to save you." He whispered. "He probably murdered his wife."

"He did *not* murder his wife." She grabbed Zane's arm and pulled him into the room. "What do you want, Zane? I hope you haven't told anyone I'm here. I'm, uh, here on official business."

His eyes popped open. "I heard in town that you were some kind of cop here to look into Wilder at the lab. But if that's not it, is the official business Katie's disappearance?"

"N-no, not really. I'm with the FBI, and I'm looking into some cold cases—not Katie's and not Raine Wilder's homicide." She pointed to the chair Michael had recently vacated, and she sat on the edge of the bed. "Is this a social call, or what?"

"Look, I understand why you wanna keep a low profile here. You were persona non grata when you and your family left. A lot of people blamed you for Katie's disappearance."

One of Natalie's eyes twitched. Not more than she blamed herself.

"Not me. I never did. You didn't make Katie do anything she didn't want to do." He scooped his hair from his eyes. "Do you have a beer or something? I just got off a twelve-hour shift, and I'm beat."

"In there." She aimed a toe at the minifridge. "Are you a doctor?"

He crouched in front of the minibar and pulled out a can of beer. "I'm a nurse."

"Why did you follow me? What do you want, Zane?"

"I never got to talk to you after Katie went missing. The cops even thought I may have had something to do with it, but I know who did it."

"You do?" Twisting her fingers in her lap, Natalie swallowed.

He dropped his chin to his chest. "I think it was a cop."

Chapter Eleven

Natalie rubbed her arms. If the thought hadn't occurred to her more than once, she would've laughed in Zane's face. "How do you know that? Do you have proof?"

He took a gulp of beer from the can. "I don't have proof. How could I have proof? I was a kid, just like you. But it was weird, right? I mean, you'd told them what happened in the forest, and they looked at her like a runaway. We knew Katie. She was not runaway material. The cops were so quick to jump on it. Then there was the evidence. Where did it all go? They combed the forest and found jack? That's hard to believe."

Evidence. It always came back to the evidence. "Stuff like that happens all the time, Zane. In my line of work, I see it all the time. Mistakes happen. What else makes you think it was the cops? That's a heavy accusation."

"It was that Reynolds guy."

"What?" The spot on her forehead where the

airbag had hit her began throbbing. "Deputy Max Reynolds?"

"Yeah, I can't stand that guy, even today, but back then he was always leering at Katie. She told me about it once."

"She never told me that." Natalie dragged a pillow into her lap and hugged it to her chest.

"Yeah, well." Zane grinned, and Natalie remembered why Katie'd had such a crush on this guy. "She told me she didn't want to tell you because she was afraid you'd say something to Reynolds and get in trouble. She said you were always so protective of her."

"She said that?" Natalie's nose tingled, and she rubbed the tip of it. "I guess so. I wish she would've told me about Reynolds, though. I think she did mention one time that she thought he was cute, but a lot of the girls felt the same way. But the rest? That's creepy."

"Anyway, when I saw you, and then someone told me you were some kind of cop here on an investigation, I knew I had to talk to you just in case you can use it." As he rose from the chair, he crushed the empty can in one hand. "Whoa! What happened to you? Your arms are all bruised."

"Had a run-in with an airbag." She squared her sore shoulders. "Look, I'd appreciate it if you didn't tell anyone my identity. Sounds like small-town gossip really gets around."

"It does." He ran a finger over the seam of his lips. "I won't say a word…as long as you let me know if you find out anything about Katie's disappearance. I'm not gonna lie. That really messed me up for a while, you know?"

"I know." She patted his arm. "Good to see you, Zane. You like nursing? Everything going well?"

"Nursing's great, and my girlfriend and I are expecting a baby in about five months. We're having a girl, and I gotta tell you, it makes me nervous around here."

"Congratulations. You'll be a great dad." She ushered him out of the hotel room without ever agreeing to keep him posted on Katie's case. He'd have to find out just like everyone else—and now, more than ever, she had every intention of solving that mystery.

THE NEXT MORNING, the rental-car company called her while she was finishing her makeup. They fell all over themselves apologizing for the brake failure and had delivered a new car to the hotel, along with the key to the conference room, which she'd left on the car's keychain. She hadn't even thought about that key last night—not that their thoughtfulness absolved the company from their total failure in providing a sufficient car. The hotel desk had the keys, and the car was gratis. That would make the FBI happy.

Natalie tossed her phone on the bed and plucked a pair of low-heeled boots out of the closet, skipping her high heels for today. Her back and neck didn't need any more stress.

She downed a couple of ibuprofen along with her breakfast in the hotel restaurant. Then she stopped by the front desk to pick up her keys to the new rental.

Her drive to the lab took longer than usual, as she kept tapping the brakes. The other drivers on the road were probably happy to see her make a turn and get out of their way.

On the way to her office, she stopped at the lunchroom to stash her leftover Indian food, which she'd have for lunch at her desk today. Next to the coffee machine, a plate of chocolate-chip cookies beckoned.

She lifted a mug from the tree, poured herself a cup of coffee, added lots of cream and dropped two cookies onto a paper plate. Nicole must've brought these in today.

As she turned with her coffee and plate in hand, she almost bumped into Dr. Butler. "Oops. Excuse me. Nearly dumped my coffee on your nice white lab coat."

"My fault." Dr. Butler pointed to the plate of

cookies. "I heard Nicole brought in her famous chocolate-chip cookies, and I couldn't get here fast enough."

Natalie slurped some of her coffee to reduce the level. "I should have some free time this afternoon, Dr. Butler. Is today a good time to visit the DNA lab?"

"Call me Rachelle and today would be great. I think Dr. Volosin is coming back tomorrow, a little earlier than I expected." Rachelle made a face.

"Send me an email, Rachelle." Natalie raised her cup to the doctor and went to her office.

When she reached the door of the conference room, she stood in front of it with her coffee cup in one hand, plate of cookies in the other and her bag hanging over her shoulder.

She was about to stoop down to place the cookies on the floor, when Jacob Reynolds came up the stairs.

"I'll hold that for you." He tucked some files under his arm and held out his hand for the plate.

"Thanks, Jacob." Natalie handed him the plate and dug her keys out of her bag. She unlocked the door and bumped it open with her hip. "You can put those down on the desk and take one for yourself. I really don't need two."

"Thanks." He swiped a cookie from the plate and took a bite that demolished half of it. With crumbs stuck to his chin, he asked, "Are there more in the lunchroom?"

"There are, but I think they're going fast." She tapped her own chin, but he didn't understand her meaning. "I meant to ask you, Jacob. Is your dad still on the job? You mentioned he was a deputy for King County."

Fourteen years ago, Jacob Reynolds would've been about six years old. What was a married man with a young child doing leering after a teenager? Maybe Zane had just been jealous. Reynolds could've just smiled at Katie at the fast-food place where she worked to send a teenage boy over the edge with despair. But Zane had told her specifically that Katie had been bothered by the cop's attention.

Was Katie right at the time? If Katie had told her about Reynolds, she probably would've gone off on the guy. She'd had no fear in those days... but those days were long gone.

Jacob finished chewing the second half of the cookie and swallowed it in a big gulp. "Yeah, my dad's still a cop. He helps out with homicides, but he's still on patrol. That's how he got me a job here. He knows a lot of people at the lab. His partner was married to Nicole Meloan. He..."

"I heard what happened. Must've upset your father."

"Yeah, Dad...well, cops don't show too much

emotion. He kept saying that Frankie never acted depressed around him. I think he felt kinda guilty that he didn't see it."

Join the club.

"I see you found the cookies," Nicole said, as she stepped into the office and brushed her fingers against her chin.

Jacob got the hint this time and rubbed the crumbs from his chin as his face turned a bright red.

Natalie's own face had warmed at the thought of Nicole catching her gossiping with the part-time gofer about her personal affairs. "I wanted to make sure I nabbed one this morning after missing out last night. Thanks again for dinner, Nicole."

"Yeah, but now I feel bad after hearing what happened to you last night."

Jacob took the opportunity to duck out of Natalie's office with a quick wave.

Natalie touched the abrasion on her forehead. "Nothing to feel bad about. The brakes could've gone out on that car at any time."

"I know, but it happened way out of town on my godforsaken little patch of land, and you went right into the forest. I can't believe you're at the office today."

"The airbag saved me, just a few bruises."

"Let me know if you need anything."

Natalie picked up the cookie. "I think I'm covered."

If Nicole had heard or been upset that Natalie had been discussing her husband with Jacob, she hadn't shown it. But now, Nicole would think her an office busybody if Natalie asked her about Max Reynolds. She must've known her husband's partner fairly well, although Frank must've been younger than Max.

Teens' perception of adult age was notoriously bad, but Natalie figured Deputy Reynolds was in his early thirties at the time of Katie's disappearance. She'd thought he was kind of cute, but old, at the time.

As she logged in to her laptop, she bit into the cookie and closed her eyes. People around here were not joking. This cookie was heaven.

The sugar and the second cup of coffee gave her a boost of energy, and she managed to complete the work on her databases outlining the evidence in all the cold cases, and any irregularities in that evidence.

The work this morning gave her the impetus to call her boss. She had to tell Jefferson about the car, anyway.

A few minutes later as she ended the phone call, Michael tapped on her open door. "I knew you'd show up. How are you feeling?"

She stretched her arms above her, linking her

fingers. "A little stiff, but otherwise, okay. Just talked to my supervisor, and he's happy with my work so far."

"Your official work. Anything on the unofficial?" He'd lowered his voice, but her office door was still open.

"Had a surprise visitor last night after you left." She put a finger to her lips. "Don't want to discuss it here, though."

"Lunch?"

"I brought in leftover Indian from last night at Nicole's." She dabbed at a cookie crumb on her plate and sucked it off her finger. "Do you think it's a good idea for us to lunch together every day?"

He sat on the edge of the desk and quirked his eyebrows up and down. "I think it's a great idea."

"Other people in the office might notice and resent it." She shoved back from the desk and massaged her neck.

"Why would they? I think they'd be happy that we're getting along because it means the lab audit is going well, and nobody is going to get blamed or lose their jobs. It's not like a competition where you're going to investigate one area and not another. I'm the head of the lab, and if I go up in flames, they all go up in flames. That's my take."

"My take is that I don't want it to appear I'm

schmoozing with the boss while investigating the lab."

"Schmoozing. Is that what we're doing? I kinda like the sound of that." He smacked the desk. "I'm going to order out and join you in here for a working lunch. Is that a good compromise? Then you can tell me all about your midnight visitor."

"Knock yourself out. It's your lab."

"I'll be back with my lunch in about thirty minutes."

"I'll be here."

When Michael left the office, Natalie pulled her access card out of her laptop and shoved it into the plastic holder hanging from the lanyard around her neck. She hadn't told Michael about the missing files, either, or the other case that had caught her eye.

If she told him about the files, she'd have to admit that she believed someone in his office was trying to sabotage her work. She'd have to confess that she'd even thought he'd done it.

Sighing, she stood up, grabbing the paper plate and coffee cup from this morning. The spasm in her back had her clenching her teeth. Time for more painkillers.

She returned to the lunchroom, washed out her coffee mug and put it on the sink to dry. Only two cookies remained from this morning, and she eyed them as she retrieved her lunch from the fridge. As she heated her foot in the microwave, she got a couple of Diet Cokes from the vending machine in case Michael forgot to order a drink with his lunch.

The microwave beeped, and she gingerly removed the plastic container with her fingertips. She threw another glance at the cookies and said, "Ah, hell."

She'd given her second cookie to Jacob, so this was just a replacement. She dropped one cookie on top of the plastic lid and hauled everything back to the conference room. She tucked the drinks under one arm, as she wrangled the key out of her pocket and into the door lock.

She didn't want to start eating without Michael, and her food needed to cool off, anyway, so she logged back in to her computer and brought up the ghost database on Katie's case.

There had been a cigarette butt found on Devil's Edge Trail the morning after Katie's disappearance, but no DNA on it. How could DNA be missing from a cigarette butt? There were also a few cigarette butts near Sierra's abandoned car—again, no DNA detected.

Odd. Usually, crime-scene investigators salivated when they found something like a cigarette butt near a body or crime scene. Even if the DNA didn't yield a match in CODIS, they still had someone's DNA.

She threaded a pen through her fingers and dropped it when Michael showed up at her door with a bag of food and two drinks in cups.

He held up the cups. "Didn't know if you had anything to drink."

She bent over to pick up the pen and tapped it against the two cans of soda. "Great minds think alike."

"Ah, but I got you the Zesty Blood Orange Diet Coke this time." He shoved the drink toward her. "If you can handle it today."

"I don't know. Indian food and Zesty Blood Orange Diet Coke." She popped the lid from her plastic container. "Sounds disgusting."

He inhaled through his nose. "That smells good. Beats my turkey on rye."

She stirred through the chicken and rice in her dish. "Nicole packed a lot in here. I'm happy to share."

"I'm good with my sandwich." He walked his swivel chair backward toward the door and closed it. "Can we talk and eat?"

"I think I can manage." She spread a piece of paper towel on her lap and got to it. "After you left last night, I mean right after, Katie's old boyfriend, Zane Tolbert, knocked on my hotel door."

Unfolding the waxy yellow paper from his sandwich, he asked, "She had a boyfriend?"

"Beginning stages." She waved her fork in the air. "Anyway, he recognized me at the Thai restaurant yesterday. I was afraid someone might see that little emo girl beneath the facade. Honestly, I'm still that little emo girl, so it's no surprise he ID'd me."

"He followed you to your hotel? That's not good."

"Zane didn't really go into how he found me at the hotel. It could've been word of mouth, local gossip." She poked at a piece of chicken. "Rumor has it that I may even be here looking into you."

Michael dropped his sandwich. "You're kidding. Jeez, people still think I did it."

"I set him straight on that, but I did admit that I might be doing a little investigating of my own into Katie's disappearance, and that's when he dropped his bombshell."

"He killed her." Michael took a big bite of his sandwich.

"No, but he thinks the cops might've had something to do with her disappearance or at least the cover-up. He said that Deputy Max Reynolds was inappropriately interested in Katie at the time, and Katie noticed. She complained to Zane about it."

"Did she ever mention it to you?"

"No. Zane said she was afraid to tell me because she thought I'd march up to Reynolds and make a scene." Her lips quivered at the corners, halfway between a smile and a grimace.

Michael walked his fingers to hers and brushed her skin, so subtle nobody would've noticed even if they were sitting at the table with them. His touch caused a little shiver to ripple across her flesh.

"I can look into Reynolds. I have a lot of connections at the sheriff's department, which pretty much saved me from going crazy when I was suspect numero uno over there."

"That would be great—as long as you're low-key."

He turned his thumbs toward his chest. "I'm the epitome of low-key."

Toying with the straw in her cup, she said, "There's something else I need to tell you."

He held up his sandwich. "Should I take this bite, or am I gonna choke on it?"

"Oh, take the bite. It's not that shocking." She took a sip of her Diet Coke,. "I had a file with Katie's case and another one with a possibly related case...and somebody stole them from this office during the fire drill the other day."

Michael swallowed his bite of sandwich and then thumped his chest with his fist. "You're kidding."

"I'm not." She shoved away the soda and cracked open the can of the other one. "That's why I was acting all unhinged about the fire drill. I think somebody set that off on purpose to get into my office and look around. They found the files and took them."

"I don't know why you just didn't tell me that in the first place." He studied her face and then slowly brushed the crumbs from his fingers. "Oh. You suspected me."

"Maybe for a brief moment." She held out her thumb and forefinger. "I didn't want to start off on the wrong foot—accusing your staff—and I'm not exactly supposed to have those files, anyway."

"I could be someone just wanted to sabotage your work, not necessarily that those files meant anything to them."

"Just? Isn't it bad enough that someone wants to sabotage my work? And why would they want to do that?"

"You know why. We've been through this already. Some people in the lab are annoyed that the FBI wants to interfere in our work."

"If the work is sloppy..." She spread her hands. "Besides, these are cold cases. We're not auditing anything recent."

"We have some old-time employees at this lab. Dr. Volosin, Lou Gray, Nicole was an intern and Felicia's been here longer than any of them, I think." He held up his hand and ticked off a finger with each name. "Some see it as an affront to their professionalism. You're FBI. You must've run into this dozens of times with dozens of departments."

"True, but nobody ever stole a file from me before, and these are files I shouldn't have in the first place. Kind of hard to report the theft."

"What's the second case? You said you took two files, Katie's and who else's?"

"Another abduction from a trail—Alma Nguyen. Even though the cops found Alma's body, the circumstances mimicked Katie's case, so it caught my eye." She glanced at the time on her laptop. "I need to wrap it up. I'm supposed to meet with Rachelle in the DNA lab this afternoon."

"Rachelle?" Michael crumpled the sandwich paper in a ball and flicked it into the plastic bag. "She went home sick."

"That's too bad. I guess I have some free time."

Her cell phone rang, and she glanced at the display. "It's the rental-car company. I hope they're not calling for more information. I told them everything I remembered."

She tapped her phone to answer. "Hello?"

"Natalie, this is Axis Rental Car Company. Do you have a minute?"

She rolled her eyes at Michael, who was busy cleaning up the trash from their lunch. "Sure. What do you need?"

"We had our mechanics do a preliminary examination of the car today. It's a good thing it didn't burn up or explode."

"That's for sure."

The woman on the phone cleared her throat. "But we do have a problem."

"A problem?"

"We won't be taking responsibility for the failure of the brakes, Natalie."

"User error? I swear I didn't stomp on them or lock them up. They just stopped working."

"N-not user error."

Natalie waited, but the pause grew uncomfortably long. "Well, that's good. What was it, then?"

"Both brake lines were cut, Natalie. Someone tampered with those brakes—on purpose."

Chapter Twelve

Something was not right on the phone. Michael kept trying to catch Natalie's eye, but she avoided his gaze and gripped the edge of the table as if afraid she'd fall over.

"I—I don't know how that would happen. I didn't do it… Yes, yes. I understand. I'll let them know."

She ended the call and sat still, the phone resting on her shoulder.

"What was that all about? What did the rental-car company say? They're trying to blame you for the accident?"

Her eyes finally focused on his face as she peeled the phone from her ear. "They said the brake lines were cut—on purpose. Somebody tampered with the car."

"What?" He dropped the plastic bag in the trash. "How does that even happen?"

Natalie jumped up suddenly. "I almost died in that crash. Do you think someone did it on purpose? Do you think someone's trying to harm me? First, the stolen files and now, the brakes."

"Wait a minute. Stolen files to hijacked brakes is a big leap. One is mischief. The other could've been deadly." He sat on the desk and folded his arms. She couldn't think that someone in this lab wanted her gone so badly they'd tampered with the brakes of her rental. "The rental-car company has had the car, a heavily damaged car, back barely one day, and they're making these claims? Sounds like they're prepping for a lawsuit coming their way. You had the car at Nicole's. Do you really think someone crept out to your car while you and Nicole were eating and cut the lines?"

"I don't know." She sucked in her bottom lip. "It could've been done before, right? Someone could've nicked the lines a little earlier in the day, at my hotel, or…here."

He downed the rest of his Diet Coke and crushed the can. "C'mon. What would be the reason behind it? Someone doesn't wanna look bad at work, so they mark you for death."

Hunching forward, she planted her hands on the table. "They had no way of knowing if or when those brakes would go out, so, no. I don't believe I've been *marked for death*, as you so elegantly put it. But what if someone just wanted to scare me off. Send me back to DC with my tail between my legs."

"Anyone who's talked to you for five minutes know that's not going to work. Look, no attorney is going to take the rental-car company's word for the failure of the brakes after they had one of their own mechanics take a cursory look...and you shouldn't, either." He brushed some crumbs from the table into his hand and tipped them in to the trash. "Is it going to scare you off?"

She tossed her hair back over her shoulder. "Of course not, but I'm going to be looking at people through a different set of eyes."

"That's a good policy, anyway." He stopped at the door and twisted his head over his shoulder. "I can check under your hood, if you like."

She raised her eyebrows. "That sounds like an improper proposal."

"I wish." He snorted as he left the office, closing the door behind him.

Michael chewed on the inside of his cheek all the way back to his office. He'd brushed off Natalie's concerns because he didn't want to worry her, but if someone in his lab was trying to run off the FBI agent, they had a real problem.

Lou Gray's name came to mind immediately. He didn't want to remind Natalie that Lou oversaw all evidence related to vehicles—evidence collection, car-crash investigations, tire tracks... and brake lines. If anyone knew how to nick a brake line for the slow release of fluid, it would be Lou.

When Michael got back to his desk, he made a call to Lou at the garage. Lou's assistant told him Lou was in the middle of overseeing the search of a drug dealer's car, knee-deep in panels, flooring and cushions.

The guy was a total professional. He had *curmudgeon* written all over him, but Michael had a hard time imagining Lou sneaking around after Natalie and tampering with her rental car. Lou would know better than anyone that that kind of tampering could be spotted in a second.

Rubbing his chin, Michael logged in to his computer and looked up Alma Nguyen's case. Alma's body was found about five months after Sierra's. Didn't share much in common with Sierra, except age, gender and approximate location of the body. Sierra had been in a car on her way home from work. Alma had been with friends in the woods, much like Katie.

Sierra had been stabbed. Alma had been shot. Just on method alone, the police were hesitant about linking the crimes, except neither crime scene yielded much evidence…or that evidence had gone missing.

As he scrolled through the file, he realized that he knew Alma's mother. Penny Nguyen worked as an accountant in town. He'd never used her services, but she'd been recommended to him on a few occasions.

He read through her interview with a tight throat, his gaze shifting to the picture of Ivy hugging Peaches. He blinked and continued reading the screen. Mrs. Nguyen had mentioned Alma's jewelry—one piece missing, replaced by a bracelet she'd never seen before.

Michael clicked through the file to find pictures of the evidence. He double-clicked the personal-items file and skipped past Alma's bloodstained clothing. Besides the clothing, items found on the body included a hair clip, a cross on a chain and gold hoop earrings. The list didn't contain a bracelet.

He flicked back to the crime-scene photo of Alma's body crumpled on the trail. He zeroed in on her hands and wrists. One sleeve of her jacket, rolled up, revealed a bare arm. The other sleeve hit the top of her hand.

He zoomed in further on her right wrist and his heart stuttered. A glint of something metal peeked out from the sleeve. It did look like a piece of jewelry.

He returned to the evidence list and went through every item again—no bracelet listed. Why had Mrs. Nguyen mentioned a bracelet and one can be seen on the photo of the body, but the evidence list didn't include it?

He logged out of his computer and grabbed his jacket. He had a sudden need for tax advice.

NATALIE JERKED UP her head at the sound of the knock. She squinted through the blinds over the conference-room window and gestured for Michael to enter.

"Are you still looking for something to do this afternoon?" His eyes were bright with excitement, which caused an answering flare in her chest.

"What did you have in mind?"

He stepped inside the room and closed the door. Tucking his hand behind him, he leaned against the door. "You mentioned the Alma Nguyen case, so I looked it up in the database."

"Okay." She dropped her pen and swiveled her chair to face him.

"In the statements, Alma's mother, Penny Nguyen, mentioned something about jewelry. Said her daughter's bracelet was missing, and that she was wearing another, unfamiliar bracelet."

Natalie's pulse ticked up a few notches. "Jewelry again. What did you discover about the bracelets?"

Parking on the edge of the desk, he said, "There was no bracelet in the list of Alma's personal items, but I looked at the pictures of her body from the crime-scene photos, and I can detect something metal around her wrist."

"Wait." She waved a hand in the air as if to clear her own confusion. "How did Alma's mother know about a bracelet if one wasn't found with the body and listed as evidence?"

"I'm not sure, but I'm about to go on a field trip and find out. Do you want to come with me to talk to Penny Nguyen? She still lives in the area." He dragged a hand through his hair. "I thought it would better if you came with me, just in case..."

"Just in case she's one of the people who believe you murdered your wife." Natalie's heart gave a painful thud.

"Exactly. If Zane Tolbert believes that, there must be others. I don't want to terrify the woman."

"I'll come with you, but first..." Natalie clicked on some files, opening the case for Sierra Conchas. "Sierra was murdered before Alma, right?"

"About five months before. Different MO. Someone shot Alma." Michael shook his head, as if trying to erase the crime-scene photo from his brain.

"Katie disappeared seven months before Sierra's homicide, lost a pendant that wound up around Sierra's neck. Was Sierra missing any jewelry?" She snapped her fingers in the air several times. "What if the MO of this guy is to take a piece of jewelry from one victim and leave it on his next? It could tie all these girls together. That's what I've been trying to find—a link between Katie's disappearance and other murders in the area."

She found the page she was looking for and leaned in to scan the personal items list. Michael hovered over her shoulder for a second pair of eyes.

He read off the list out loud. "A number of stud earrings along her ear down to the lobe, several bangles on her arm, some of which fell off in the struggle, and the witches'-knot pendant, which we know didn't belong to her. Did anyone report that Sierra was missing anything at the time of her death."

"I didn't see that anywhere, but it's not hard to imagine that her killer took one of those bangles without anyone noticing and slipped it over Alma's hand." She tapped her fingers on the desk. "But if that happened, where is it? Why isn't it listed in the evidence of Alma's personal effects?"

"That's what I'm hoping Mrs. Nguyen can tell us." Michael wagged his finger at the screen. "Get to the photos of Sierra's personal effects and get a picture on your phone of those bracelets."

While Natalie followed his instructions, Michael took two long strides to the coat-tree and plucked her jacket and purse from it. "Got it?"

"Give me a few seconds." Once she'd snapped a picture of the bracelets, she logged off her laptop and pushed back from the desk. "Do you know where to find Mrs. Nguyen?"

"I do."

"What's your story going to be?"

"Me?" He tapped his chest. "I'm there for tax advice. You're there to ask her about Alma."

"You're going to make me the bad guy?" She jerked open the door and almost ran into Lou Gray, who was charging down the hallway. "Oops, sorry."

Lou ignored her and tipped his chin at Michael. "Heard you were looking for me."

"It can wait. Find anything in the drug dealer's vehicle yet?"

"Oh, yeah." Lou rubbed his hands together. Then his gaze darted from Michael to Natalie. "We'll catch up later."

Lou saluted as he ambled toward the lunchroom.

As they went downstairs, Natalie asked in a low voice, "You called Lou? What for?"

"About your rental-car brakes."

She tripped on the last step, and Michael caught her arm. "You don't suspect him, do you?"

"I'm not going to come at him like that, but I wanted to judge his response."

"He'll see right through you." Natalie waved

to Sam as they breezed out the front door. "Your car or mine?"

"No offense, but I'd rather drive."

She punched him in the arm. "Not my fault."

They drove to Penny Nguyen's house, situated in a neat tract of homes, settled near the town. No two-lane roads, no tunnel of towering trees, no animals darting into the street.

Michael parked on the street in front of a tidy, white picket fence with a wooden sign on the gate. Blue lettering on the sign advertised CPA/ Taxes.

Natalie lifted the latch on the gate. "If she has a client, you're out of luck."

"I'll take my chances. We're nowhere near tax season, although the end of the year always puts me in a panic, looking for receipts and looking for investments to lower my taxes." Michael followed her through the gate, their footsteps crunching the dry leaves, and up to the front door.

When she reached the porch, she stood to the side, allowing Michael access to the front door and the doorbell, which was connected to a camera. She murmured, "She might not let you in once she sees you."

"Thanks for the vote of confidence." He pressed the doorbell with his thumb.

Whether or not Mrs. Nguyen checked the

camera, she opened the door almost immediately and smiled, the lines crinkling at the corners of her eyes making her look a lot jollier than she had a reason to look. The gray streaks in her hair gleamed beneath the light from the house. "Hello. Can I help you?"

Michael took an audible breath. "Mrs. Nguyen, I'm Dr. Michael Wilder. I work for the Washington State Patrol at the forensics lab here in town."

She dipped her head. "I know who you are, Dr. Wilder. I followed your wife's case, and I'm very sorry for your...troubles."

"Thank you, Mrs. Nguyen, and you can call me Michael."

"I'm Penny." She tilted her head, birdlike, her face tightening over her delicate bone structure. "Something tells me you're not here for tax advice. You'd better come in."

She widened her door, and Michael waved Natalie in first. "I'm sorry. This is FBI Special Agent Natalie Brunetti."

Penny closed the door and locked the dead bolt. "Now, I *know* you're not here for financial advice. I'd actually heard about Agent Brunetti's presence in town and her accident last night."

Natalie whistled. "The rumor mill in Marysville is alive and well, and I'm Natalie."

She stuck out her hand, and Penny took it in a

surprisingly firm grip for such a petite woman. "Tea, anyone? I always find it helps for tough conversations."

Natalie exchanged a glance with Michael. This woman was prescient. "Yes, please."

Penny invited them to sit down and went into the kitchen to prepare their tea.

Seated on the couch next to Michael, Natalie leaned over, bumped his shoulder and whispered, "You'd abandoned the tax story as soon as you saw her, didn't you?"

"I couldn't lie to her, not after seeing the pain in her face. It's still there, isn't it? Her clients probably don't see it, but you and I know the look. We've had the look."

Natalie gave his hand a surreptitious squeeze before bounding up from the couch to help Penny with an elaborate tea tray.

Once they were settled, Penny held her cup to her lips, her pinkie finger raised. "Now, what do you want to know about Alma's death?"

Natalie almost choked on her first sip of tea. Did Penny still have hope that they'd find her daughter's killer? This woman made Natalie even more determined to dig in and see this through. She had no intention of leaving Marysville until she got to the bottom of these homicides. She didn't believe she could solve them on her own, or even with Michael's help, but just maybe she could get another investigation started—one that would look at these three cases together.

Natalie daintily dabbed her lips with a napkin. "I'm here to look into evidence for several cold cases. Alma's isn't one of them, but I've seen some similarities between hers and some others."

"Sierra Conchas and that poor girl Katie Fellows, who disappeared."

This time Natalie almost dropped her cup in her lap. She put it down in the saucer with a clink. "How do you know that, Penny?"

Penny smiled sadly. "Call it mother's intuition. I tried telling Detective Morse, who was on my daughter's case, and that Deputy Reynolds, but they wrote me off as a grief-stricken parent, which I was."

Michael glanced around the room. "Is Mr. Nguyen still with you?"

"He's still with someone, but it isn't me." Penny gripped the arms of her chair. "After Alma's murder, my husband, my ex, he went off the rails. I redirected my grief by conducting my own investigation. He redirected his into the bottle. I'd finally had enough of his drinking and kicked him out. He moved to Hawaii. Still drinking, I think."

"I'm sorry, Penny." Michael hunched forward,

his elbows on his knees. "A homicide is hell on everyone left behind."

"It is." Her dark eyes bright with unshed tears, Penny asked, "How's your little girl?"

"She's fine."

Michael seemed to handle accusations better than sympathy, so he rose from the couch and studied some photos of Alma on a bookshelf. "Pretty girl. Was she good at the piano?"

"Alma was good at everything...except self-preservation. She trusted everyone." Penny dropped her gaze to her hands folded in her lap.

Natalie gave Michael a glance from the corner of her eye, and he nodded. She took a deep breath through her nose. "Penny, in your interview with the police, you mentioned that Alma was wearing a piece of jewelry at the time of her death, something you'd never seen her with before. What was it?"

Penny's head shot up and she encircled her wrist with her fingers. "A bracelet, one of those circles without a catch. A bangle, you'd call it. Alma never wore those kinds of bracelets. Her wrists were too small, and the bangles wouldn't stay on.

Natalie slipped her phone from her purse and tapped the picture of Sierra's bracelets. Licking her dry lips, she crouched beside Penny's chair and held out the phone. "Did it look like any of these?"

Penny gasped and grabbed the phone, tugging it from Natalie's hand. She held it close to her face, staring at the display from behind her glasses. "Just like this one."

Chapter Thirteen

Penny's hand trembled when she handed the phone back to Natalie. "Where did you find it?"

"I-it's not the one you saw on Alma, but how did you know about the bracelet on Alma's arm? It's not listed in her file. There's no other mention of it except in your interview with Deputy Reynolds."

"When that couple found Alma's body on the trail, she'd been missing overnight. My husband and I were out all day looking for her, questioning her friends. My husband had a police scanner in the car. We heard about the discovery of a body, a young woman, and we arrived there almost the same time as the police." Penny removed her glasses and rubbed her eyes. "I saw my baby lying in the dirt, blood soaking the ground around her head like a halo. An angel in life, and an angel in death. They couldn't stop me. They couldn't hold me back. I ran to her. Even in my frantic despair, I knew enough not to touch her, not to interfere with any evidence, but I saw the bracelet then. I noticed it because I thought it was a handcuff, but when I looked close, I could see it was a silver bangle, imprinted with little flowers…like the ones you just showed me."

Michael crossed the room and dropped onto the couch, as if his legs couldn't support him anymore. He croaked, his voice rough. "You never saw that bracelet again?"

Penny shook her head. "No. I told them about the bracelet, but they acted like they didn't know what I was talking about. I asked them why she had a bracelet that didn't belong to her. They dismissed me, but I knew what I saw. I-is it important?"

"It could be." Michael placed their cups on the tea tray.

"Penny." Natalie sat on the floor at Penny's feet. "You said Alma had a piece of her own jewelry missing. What was that?"

"That was a bracelet, too, but not that type. Alma had bought a bracelet at a Native American fair—a pretty, delicate thing with seed pearls and little sea turtles and beads. She wore it every day since the day she bought it." A shudder rant through Penny's slight frame. "That bracelet wasn't on her body, and I never saw it again. So her killer replaced one bracelet with another."

The silence hung in the room until Michael

broke it. "Penny, can I ask you not to say anything to anyone about this?"

She snorted softly. "Whom would I tell? My husband is gone. Alma's brother is a doctor in Boston and hates it here. The friends I have left don't want to hear about my tragedy. I'll keep it to myself."

Natalie patted Penny's knee. "We'll get to the bottom of this. I promise."

As Michael carried the dishes to the kitchen, Natalie collected her coat and purse. "One more thing, Penny. Did Alma ever mention Deputy Reynolds before?"

Penny had risen to her feet a bit unsteadily and kept the back of her knees pressed against the cushion of the chair for support. "Not really. I know he had given some talks at the high school about drugs when Alma had been a student there a few years earlier. The girls at the time had thought he was cute, but that was before Alma's murder. Why?"

Michael emerged from the kitchen and cleared his throat. "We're looking at all the deputies on the cases, the ones who managed the evidence. We may have to talk to them again."

Penny put her hand on her hip, not quite buying it. "I see. I won't say a word, Michael, about any of it."

They thanked her for her time and left the house as Penny stood on the porch and watched them.

Natalie scooped in a big breath of pine-scented air. "Intense."

Penny lifted her hand. "Give your little girl a hug."

Michael waved back, and they got into the car. Michael clenched the steering wheel for several seconds before starting the car. "That poor woman."

"Michael." Natalie tugged on his sleeve. "It seems like this killer had some jewelry exchange going on. This was his MO, and it connects Katie, Sierra and Alma. He took a piece from one girl and left it on his next victim."

They pulled away from Penny's home. "We don't know if he left anything with Katie because she's the one who's never been found."

"Perhaps Katie was his first. Maybe seeing that pendant around Katie's neck is what gave him the idea, but my guess is that if her body is ever found there will be a piece of unfamiliar jewelry with her."

"I hope that happens one day—for her family's sake as well as yours." He gave her knee a quick squeeze and made a turn. Dusk had already settled, painting the horizon with orange streaks. "I'm starving. Are you hungry?"

"I could use a bite to eat before you drop me

off at the lab. Don't forget. My car's there, and I left my laptop, too." She twisted in her seat to face him. "Wait. Can I get into the lab without a key after hours? If not, we'd better go straight back there."

"You don't need a key, just your temp badge. Miles is the nighttime security guard. I'll bring you back and let him know you need to get inside."

He turned off the main road, and she tapped the window. "I thought we were going back to town to get something to eat."

"My house comes first. We can eat something there."

"Oh." She twisted her fingers in her lap. "Are your sister and daughter going to be home? Won't it be an imposition on your sister?"

"They'll be there, and my sister doesn't care about rules of etiquette. I could bring an army home for dinner, and she wouldn't blink an eye. She'd just reach for the phone and my credit card and order in."

"Maybe you should call her, anyway. Give her a heads-up."

"Too late." Michael pulled down a lane with a row of trees on either side, but the road was well-groomed, and other houses, or at least their mailboxes, made an appearance every 200 hundred feet or so. Far enough apart to maintain the

Carol Ericson   173

woodsy, bucolic atmosphere of the neighborhood but close enough for shouting…in case someone needed help.

Instead of the unrelenting darkness that surrounded Nicole's area, this place had twinkling garden lights and the yellow glow from windows from the house set back from the street.

Natalie exhaled. "It's beautiful here. Spacious but cozy at the same time, if that makes sense."

"You're right. Most of our backyards are connected by a trail that winds through the woods with gates between the properties. In the summer, we'll leave our gates open to each other's yards and we'll have a barbecue across a couple of lawns." His jaw tightened. "Not much of that this past summer."

Did his own neighbors suspect him of Raine's murder? Penny Nguyen proved that the whole town didn't believe him guilty. His coworkers didn't, either, judging by the way they respected him.

He turned into one of the driveways, where a white mailbox entwined with purple vines sat at the edge. "Circular driveway and everything—not that I've been able to take advantage of that since my sister moved in."

He pulled behind an old VW van, the back painted with curlicue flowers. Michael said, "Molly parks that in the driveway at an angle as if it were an abandoned car. She *should* abandon that car. I won't let her take Ivy out in that van. The thing could break down at any minute."

Michael's house fit into its surroundings seamlessly, with its cedar-shake siding and natural stone accents at the base of the house and around the wide porch. Two large windows looked out onto a garden, which was riotous with color, pinwheels and mermaids. A wooden bench sat on one edge of the garden, with a yellow cushion added for comfort—the perfect spot to read. A shadow passed in front of the window, and a little knot formed in Natalie's stomach.

As they got out of the car, a young woman with long black hair flying behind her tripped down the porch to meet them. She gave Natalie a sweet smile, but her smooth face had a furrow between her eyebrows. "Am I glad to see you. I didn't want to bother you at work, but I was just about to call your cell."

Michael slammed the driver's-side door and strode toward his sister. "Is Ivy okay?"

"Yeah, I'm sorry to scare you. Ivy's fine, but…" Molly craned her head over her shoulder to glance at the house behind her.

"What is it, Molly?"

The edge to Michael's voice only made Molly's smile wider. "It's probably nothing. Is this the FBI person who's making your life hell."

Michael grunted. "Natalie, this is my thoroughly annoying, but indispensable sister, Molly. And I never told her you were making my life hell."

Molly thrust out her hand. "I'm just kidding. Nice to meet you, Natalie. Are you joining us for dinner?"

"I'm sorry we're just dropping in on you like this. Please don't go to any trouble."

"Moi?" Molly's hair was fashioned into a low chignon with a few twists and tucks. "I never do. Ask Michael. If you can handle some leftover spaghetti, I got you covered."

"Whatever is honestly fine with me." Natalie spread her hands. "And I'm sorry I don't have anything to bring. This was totally last-minute. We were out working, and Michael has to take me back to the lab for my car and laptop."

Molly threw up her hands and aimed a broad wink at Michael. "You don't have to explain anything to me."

Poking his sister in the back, Michael said, "Now, can we get inside, and you can tell me why you were so anxious for me to come home."

Natalie hung back, allowing brother and sister to enter the house before her. The scent of warm vanilla permeated the air, and it didn't take long for Natalie to see that a candle, and not the oven, was the source of the aroma.

"Daddy!"

Natalie's gaze traveled to the little girl standing up and holding on to the edge of a playpen, a giant area outfitted with blocks, stuffed animals, dolls and books. Michael's blue eyes stared out from the little round face, but any other resemblance to her father ended there. Soft brown hair framed Ivy's face, glowing with peaches and cream and happiness. She didn't look like a little girl missing her mommy, just one incredibly pleased to see her daddy.

Michael's strides ate up the space between them, and he swooped in and lifted her in the air. Ivy giggled and splayed her arms and legs out, as if trying to fly.

Natalie pressed a hand to her heart. "She's adorable."

Molly stood beside Natalie and bumped her shoulder. "I know. Pretty hard to believe with a moody dad and a nut-job mom."

Molly had lowered her voice on her last words, but Michael shot her a scowl as if he'd heard.

Michael brought Ivy close to his chest and kissed the top of her head. "What have you been doing today?"

Ivy twisted her body and pointed to the large picture window that looked out onto a grassy backyard with a swing set and massive trees that signaled the beginning of the forest. The view must be breathtaking during the light of day.

"Peaches, Daddy. Peaches."

"Peaches went away, my peapod." Michael rubbed Ivy's back as he rolled his eyes at Molly.

"That's what I was going to tell you, Michael. I was sitting on the couch on my laptop looking up my friend's exhibit in Portland while Ivy was playing, and she started yelling Peaches's name and pointing outside." Molly crossed to the window and placed a hand against the glass. "I looked but didn't see anything, or maybe I just saw some bushes shaking. So I went outside and called for Peaches. I even walked into the yard. I did hear noise in the underbrush that sounded like an animal, but I'm not going out in the wild to check—besides, I had Ivy inside."

"Maybe Ivy just saw a small dog and her brain went straight to *her* small dog." He bounced Ivy in his arms. "Did you see a doggy outside?"

Her blue eyes grew round and sparkled with excitement like Michael's did. "Peaches. Peaches outside."

"I hate to give you any more work, Molly, but I think I'm going to have to get another dog." He tapped Ivy on the nose. "Would you like that, Ivy? Another doggy?"

Her face crumpled and grew red. "Peaches."

"Michael." Molly put her hand on his arm

and tickled Ivy under the chin at the same time. "Could you just go look outside to be sure? She seemed convinced and would not give it up."

"She's two and a half, Molly. Any small dog is going to look the same to her."

"Then go out there and make sure there's not some other dog wandering around." She gave Michael a shove and held out her arms for Ivy.

Ivy clambered into Molly's arms.

Michael raised an eyebrow at Natalie. "Care to join me in the great dog hunt?"

"Absolutely. I think I can still tell the difference between a fox and a dog."

Michael brushed past Natalie on the way to the kitchen and opened a cupboard. "I have a flashlight. Molly, turn on the outdoor lights."

Natalie hadn't removed her jacket when she'd come inside, so she tugged it around her and followed Michael out to the backyard, now lit up. The smell of roses and rain tempered the sharp scent of the pines, which could be overpowering. Truly a slice of civilization amid the untamed forest.

Michael clicked on the flashlight and the strong beam swept across the edge of the grass and along the tree line. The light picked up the shared community trail that wended through the underbrush before plunging into the woods.

Michael whistled. "Peaches. Oh, P-e-e-eaches. C'mon, girl. You out here?"

He replaced the whistle with kissing sounds that would've definitely had Natalie come running. A smile curving her lip, she crept closer to the trees, their leaves shivering in the light breeze and touched by the icy beam from the flashlight.

She whispered the dog's name. "Peaches."

Something rustled beyond the trail, and Natalie hissed at Michael. "I hear something."

He joined her and aimed his light at the area where she'd heard the noise. "Peaches."

An animal whimpered, and they looked at each other. Natalie said the obvious first. "That sounded like a dog to me."

"Could be a fox." As he scanned the ground with the light, it picked up a pair of gleaming eyes.

Natalie grabbed his arm, her fingers digging in. "Right there."

"Peaches?"

A small dog hurtled out of the bushes, yapping and dancing around Michael's ankles.

Natalie sank to her knees in the wet grass and reached for the wriggling pug. "Is it her? Is it Peaches?"

"My God." Michael's mouth had dropped

open. "It's really you. It's really Peaches, after all this time."

He dropped to the grass beside Natalie, handing her the flashlight, and scooped up Peaches. He buried his nose in the dog's filthy fur. "She's still wearing her collar."

As Natalie illuminated the collar, Michael hooked his finger around it. "Looks like her tag might've come off."

"Are you sure?" Natalie squinted and peered at the collar, which must've been pink at one time. "I see something glittering on the collar. Maybe the tag got bent or something."

Michael stroked Peaches as he tugged on her collar. "There's something caught on it. It's not her tag."

Something jingled as he untangled the object from the collar. When he had it cupped in his hand, he choked. "No."

"What is it, Michael?" She wedged the flashlight between her knees, aiming it at Michael's hand, and hovered over the shiny object in his palm. "Oh, my God. It can't be. It can't be the same."

"It has to be, Natalie." He dangled the pretty bracelet from his fingers. "It's Alma Nguyen's bracelet. The one taken from her dead body."

Chapter Fourteen

Michael sat on the grass, Peaches's emaciated body in his arms and the dew soaking through the seat of his pants. He felt none of it until Natalie shouted in his face.

"Michael! What does this mean? Why does Peaches have Alma's bracelet from twelve years ago?"

Molly called from the house. "Did you two get lost out there or is there some hanky-panky going on?"

Michael closed his fist around the bracelet and held a finger to his lips. "Not a word about this to Molly…or anyone else. Not until we sort it out."

Natalie started to talk, but he gripped her wrist before she could say anything. "I don't understand, either, but we can't discuss it now."

He slipped the bracelet into his pocket, where it burned like a living thing, and he pushed up from the soggy grass with Peaches under one arm.

As he marched back to the house, he felt Natalie slip her finger in his belt loop, as if she needed something to keep her steady. Her touch anchored him, too, and he cleared his throat as he approached the house.

"Ivy was right. Never doubt a toddler." He held up Peaches, and Molly squealed.

"That's Peaches? She came home."

Molly ran to pluck up Ivy from her playpen, and Ivy smiled from ear to ear, repeating Peaches's name and patting the dog on the head. At one point, Ivy looked up at Michael. "Mama?"

The lump in Michael's throat proved too big for words to slip past it, so Molly combed her fingers through Ivy's hair and said, "Mama's not coming home."

Ivy hugged the little pug, smooshing her face into her fur. Michael would worry about fleas later. He could barely think straight, and he had three people eying him for answers.

Molly chewed on the side of her thumb, a habit she'd inherited from Mom. "You're going to have to tell the police, Michael. This is huge."

His sister had no idea how huge.

"I realize that."

"You might even need to tell them before you wash the dog. I mean, you don't want to destroy any evidence, do you?" Molly grabbed her phone from the coffee table and snapped several pictures of Peaches. "Just in case."

He closed his eyes. He'd already removed the

biggest piece of evidence from Peaches's collar. "Peaches has been gone for over six months. She's not going to yield any evidence worth having."

Molly tapped her chin. "I get it—rain, dirt, mud. It would've destroyed any evidence from the, uh, thing."

Michael cuddled Ivy in his arms, while she cuddled an exhausted Peaches in hers. He caught Natalie's reflection in the window, her face a while oval. She hadn't recovered from the shock yet, but in all the excitement Molly hadn't noticed Natalie's demeanor.

"I need to get Natalie back to the lab, so she can get her car and her laptop, and we never even fed her."

"Don't worry about me. I'll figure out something. I can order a car on my phone to take me back."

Molly jumped up from the floor. "Michael, don't make her do that. I can take care of everything here. Ivy and I will give Peaches a bath and feed her. Do you have any dog food left?"

"Not any of the dry stuff, but I'm sure there are a few cans in the cupboard in the garage over the washer and dryer." Michael left Ivy on the floor with Peaches and brushed off the knees of his pants. "I don't want to dump all of this on you, Molly. Are you sure?"

"Positive. Just go take Natalie back, and then

you can help me when you return. Ivy will be my assistant." Molly ducked down and ruffled the top of Ivy's hair.

After they settled everything with Molly, Michael walked with Natalie back to his car in silence. Neither of them spoke until he'd backed the car out of the driveway and hit the road.

Then Natalie went off like a teakettle. "What the hell just happened? First the dog that was with your wife when she was murdered returns home after six months, and if that weren't astounding in and of itself, the dog has a dead woman's bracelet attached to her collar. Michael, tell me you're thinking what I'm thinking. Or am I losing my mind?"

"If you are, I'm right there with you. The person who murdered Alma thirteen years ago and stole her bracelet is still at large, and he killed my wife. The reason Raine wasn't found with this bracelet is because it somehow got tangled with Peaches's collar, or Peaches somehow got it from Raine's body, or..." He slammed his hands against the steering wheel.

Natalie put her fingers to her lips. "Or the killer attached that bracelet to Peaches's collar."

"Wait. We don't know for sure." Michael clapped a hand on his forehead. "Maybe that's not even Alma's bracelet. We just talked to

Penny. We had that bracelet in our heads, and it materialized."

"Yeah, a Native American-style bracelet with seed pearls and sea turtles. That's just so common."

Michael lifted his shoulders, desperate for something to make sense. "Alma bought it at a Native American fair. They could've sold others."

"Those must be some bad-luck bracelets, then." She snorted. "Of course, it's Alma's bracelet, Michael, and Raine's murder is connected to the others."

"That's impossible. It's been too long since his previous murder." His foot had been coming down on the accelerator, and he took the last turn way too fast. He eased off the pedal and loosened his grip on the steering wheel, flexing his fingers.

"We don't know that. He could've been operating in another area. He could've been in prison. You know the score. It's all too coincidental."

"Raine is out of his age demographic. She was thirty, she had a child. She was strangled, for God's sake. The other two were stabbed and shot." Michael's hand shook as he snatched up the water bottle in the cup holder.

Natalie took the bottle from him and unscrewed the cap. "Let's see what Penny has to say about that bracelet. If she verifies that it belonged to Alma, will you believe Raine's murder is connected to Alma's and the others?"

"I guess I'd have to. There's no way Peaches just happened to get tangled up with Alma's bracelet thirteen years after her murder. Peaches didn't even disappear in the same area as Alma was discovered." Michael took the turn toward the lab. "Where was she? How did she survive out there? It doesn't look like someone had found her or was taking care of her."

"Six months is a long time. Someone must've been feeding her. If she could only talk."

Natalie tapped her fingers against her chin. "If this is the same killer, he would've taken a piece of jewelry from Raine. I mean, why change your MO when you're trying to make a comeback. Was Raine missing any jewelry? Wedding ring?"

Michael spit out a breath. "She'd stopped wearing that, months before her death. You'd have to ask her boyfriend, RJ."

Michael pulled into the parking lot of the lab sooner than he would've liked. He and Natalie still had so much to discuss, but he had to go home to his little girl and try to explain why Peaches had returned, but her mother hadn't.

NATALIE HAD TO convince Michael that he didn't have to wait for her to collect her things from the office. She could tell he was anxious to get back to Ivy, and he'd already waved to Miles to let her into the building. Several stray cars remained in the parking lot, so there had to be a few late-night stragglers.

Once inside, she strode toward the security desk and introduced herself to Miles. "Is there a cut-off point when the office closes? I'd like to do a little work while I'm here."

"You can work here all night, if you like. Some do." He tapped the desk. "You need to check out when you're leaving, though, and exit through the front doors. I have to know who's in the building."

"Got it. Thanks, Miles."

She made a detour to the lunchroom on the way back to her office. She never did get that leftover spaghetti at Michael's house, but she did get something much more important. Could Katie's abductor and presumed killer be back in Marysville, determined to pick up where he left off?

Had Raine been missing any jewelry when her body was discovered.=? That seemed like a very important point right now, but she wasn't about to interrupt his family time to ask him. What kind of killer took a thirteen-year break? Like she'd told Michael earlier—an ex-con, someone in the military, someone who'd recently returned to the area.

She inserted her debit card into the vending machine and punched a button for a bag of chips and a bottle of water. She collected her dinner and returned to the conference room. On her way, she didn't see any other employees in their offices or cubicles, but they could be in their labs.

As she let herself into the room, her gaze swept the area, looking for anything out of place. Even though she'd locked up every day since getting the key, something always felt off in this conference room.

She dove back into her databases and added the details about Sierra's bangle, the photo of Alma's body showing a bracelet on her wrist and Penny's assertion that Alma was also missing a bracelet. Then Natalie held her breath and created another file for Raine Wilder.

Michael had the bracelet wrapped around Peaches's collar in his possession, but Molly hadn't been the only one taking pictures tonight. Natalie had a couple of photos of the bracelet on her phone. She could send it to Penny right now and clear up any doubt...not that she had any.

Michael needed to know, too. The truth would bring him out of his denial that his wife's murder was connected to the other homicides. The link would only benefit him, as it would completely establish his innocence.

Now, they just somehow had to convince the

police. Nobody knew the necklace found on Sierra belonged to the missing Katie, and that was her fault because she'd never told the police that Katie was wearing her pendant. Sierra's mother hadn't seen the necklace before, but that didn't mean anything. How many teenage girls hid items of jewelry or clothing from their parents?

Sierra wore so many bangles on her arm, nobody would've known if one were missing, and nobody but Penny could attest to an unknown bracelet around Alma's wrist. The bracelet hadn't even been logged in the evidence. And who was going to believe a mother who'd been grieving for thirteen years that her daughter's missing bracelet was found on the dog of another murder victim?

All she and Michael had was hearsay, supposition, disgruntled parents looking for justice, a suspect in his wife's murder and a lying FBI agent. They also had a cop who'd been too close to the victims and the crime scenes. Maybe Michael could talk to Max Reynolds about Alma's bracelet. Michael would be telling the sheriff's department about the return of Peaches, and he'd have to mention the bracelet. Whether he told him his suspicion about the bracelet was another matter.

She leaned back in her chair and popped open the bag of chips. She stuffed a few in her mouth and cracked open her water, then wiped her greasy fingers on a napkin. She pulled out her phone and tapped on the picture of the seed pearl bracelet. Then she texted the picture to Penny along with the million-dollar question.

She placed the phone on the desk and stared at it while she continued to crunch through the chips. As she tipped the crumbs from the empty bag in her mouth, she heard her phone buzz. Letting the bag drop to the floor, she lunged for her phone. The first two words of Penny's text slammed against her heart.

It's hers.

A million thoughts rushed through her brain at once, causing a severe crossing of wires. She squeezed her eyes shut and forced herself to breathe in and out, slowly. Then she opened her eyes and read through the questions in Penny's text, none of which she could answer right now.

She did her best to placate Penny, and herself, before packing up her laptop. She had to break the news to Michael, but in his heart, he already knew the truth, just as she'd known it.

She gulped down the rest of the water and tossed the chip bag in the trash, and the water bottle in the blue recycling bin. She could always order some room service if she felt hungry when she got back to the hotel, but she didn't think she'd be able to eat the rest of the night. A drink, maybe.

She rubbed her hands together, still feeling the residue from the chips. She'd make a quick trip to the ladies' room to wash her hands before going back to the hotel. She left her stuff in the conference room and headed toward the bathrooms next to the lunchroom.

She pushed on the door, but it wouldn't budge. She bumped it with her hip but got the same result. Maybe the janitorial staff locked up the bathrooms at night, but that didn't make sense if people were working here. Maybe they locked up certain bathrooms.

Natalie leaned over the staircase railing that looked into the lobby to ask Miles, but he must've been on rounds. All the labs were downstairs, and it made sense if the bathrooms in the lobby stayed unlocked. Made sense for Miles to keep track of the people in the building, too.

She jogged downstairs and swung to the right for the hallway leading to the restrooms. The fluorescent lights above flickered but never went on completely. She should've just brought her stuff with her to save a trip back upstairs.

This time when she pushed on the door, it eased open with a creak. A tiled wall separated the door from the rest of the bathroom, and she skirted it and parked herself in front of the mirror.

She patted her hair, which had frizzed out from all the moisture in Michael's backyard. There was only so much she could do with her curls in this weather. She even had a smudge of dirt on her chin, which nobody had bothered to tell her about, and the bruises on her arms from the airbag had reached the dark purple stage.

Sighing, she cranked on the faucet and squirted some soap into her palm. She lathered up her hands under the water and rinsed them clean, even rubbing the dirt spot on her chin.

When she removed her hands from beneath the faucet, the water stopped, and she turned to yank a paper towel from the dispenser. She reached for a second and froze, as she heard a creak from the door.

Holding the paper towel from her fingertips, she looked at her reflection in the mirror, her wide eyes staring back at her. A shuffling noise and another creak had her spinning around, but she couldn't see the door due to the privacy wall.

If someone wanted to use the bathroom, why didn't she just come in? Maybe it was Miles or the cleaning crew. She crumpled the paper in her hands and called out. "Hello?"

A hooded figure appeared at the corner of the wall, and Natalie screamed.

Chapter Fifteen

The man at the door flicked his hood back from a head of silver hair and growled. "Who the hell are you?"

Natalie put a hand to her throat where her pulse fluttered wildly. "Who are *you*? You're in the ladies' room."

"Yeah, because I heard noises in here."

"Yeah, because it's a bathroom with running water and everything." Natalie's fear was beginning to turn to annoyance.

And then Miles's broad frame appeared behind the silver-haired man. "Oh, hello, Dr. Volosin. Everything okay in here? Thought I heard someone screaming."

Dr. Volosin, the DNA lab manager. Natalie narrowed her eyes.

Volosin jabbed a finger at her. "She screamed. Who the hell is she, and what's she doing near our labs?"

Natalie fired her balled-up paper towel at the trash can and missed. "I'm FBI Special Agent

Natalie Brunetti, and I'm in this ladies' room because the one upstairs near my office is locked."

"My bad." Miles patted his chest. "Should've warned you, Natalie. The cleaning crew locks up all the bathrooms at night except the ones down here. Everything okay now?"

"Fine. Thanks for checking, Miles." She bent over and swept the paper towel from the floor.

When Miles left, Volosin leaned his tall, wiry frame against the tile wall. "I thought Nat Brunetti was a man."

Spreading her arms out to her sides, she said, "Clearly not. Why are you dressed like a burglar?"

He tugged on his hooded sweatshirt. "Just came off a cross-country flight. I dress for comfort after wearing suits at the conference all week. What are you doing here at this hour?"

"I could ask you the same thing. You came straight to the lab from the airport?" She crossed her arms. She felt sorry for Rachelle working for this disagreeable person. Why didn't he leave?

"After being away all week, I have a lot of work to finish up." He crossed his arms, mimicking her. "You might've heard. The Feds are doing an audit on this lab."

"Yeah, I had heard. I also heard that you've been working at this lab for almost twenty years."

"That's right. Long enough to have worked on

your cold cases—Collette, David, Lizzie, Aaron, Sierra…and Katie." Volosin winked and slipped out of the bathroom, leaving her mouth gaping open like a fish's.

How had he known she was looking into Katie's disappearance? The others had been on the FBI's audit notification to the lab, but not Katie. No wonder Rachelle had wanted to meet with her in the lab before Volosin returned, and now, they'd missed their chance.

Natalie left the bathroom without even glancing in the direction of the labs. When she got to the conference room, she checked that everything was in place. Why had Volosin brought up Katie's case? How had he known?

She'd stayed longer than she'd intended. Ivy would probably be in bed by now. She tapped her phone to call Michael and almost hung up after four rings, but he answered, out of breath. "Are you alright? Did you make it back to the hotel okay?"

"I'm still at the office. How's Ivy doing? Did she settle down?"

"Fast asleep with Peaches on the floor beside her. We did give her a thorough bath—Peaches, not Ivy—and she looks healthy if a little underweight. No wounds or anything like that. She somehow survived out there before making her way home." He let out a long, raspy breath.

"I'm not gonna lie. It's been tough on Ivy having Peaches come back and not her mother."

"It must be so confusing for her...and you." Natalie doodled on the pad in front of her. "Look, Michael. I made an executive decision and called Penny Nguyen about the bracelet, sent her a text with a picture I took."

"And." His voice sounded tight, and she hated to add to his distress.

"Penny confirmed that the bracelet is Alma's. There's no doubt now that Raine's murder is linked to the others." She stopped breathing until he replied.

"I guess that's it then. I'll be giving Detective Ibarra an earful tomorrow when I tell him Peaches returned with a dead girl's bracelet wound around her collar."

"I was just thinking about that tonight. We really don't have any proof of anything, do we?"

"We have a photo of Alma's dead body with a bracelet on her wrist that wasn't recorded in evidence. This is exactly what you're looking at, Natalie. Someone dropped the ball." He cleared his throat. "You're going to have to come clean, though. You have to declare your connection to the Katie Fellows's case because you'll have to explain how you know the pendant on Sierra Conchas belonged to Katie."

"I can't do that, Michael. I'll be removed from

this investigation, and we'll never find out what happened. We can work around that bit of information. Sierra's mother insisted she'd never seen the pendant before, so it must've come from the killer."

"That's a big leap. Do you want to come over to my place tomorrow when I call Detective Ibarra? I'm sure he's going to want to come by to look at the dog and ask questions. We can lay things out for him then."

"I was supposed to meet Rachelle in the DNA lab tomorrow, but her boss, Dr. Volosin, came back tonight. Do you know if Rachelle is coming in tomorrow, or is she still sick?"

"I haven't heard from her yet. So you met Phil Volosin."

"He came straight to the lab from the airport."

"He does that a lot."

"He's obnoxious."

Michael chuckled. "He can be abrasive, but he does a good job. He was the keynote speaker at that conference."

"And yet…" Natalie clicked her tongue. "He was at the forensics lab when all these issues occurred."

"I don't believe any of the issues involved DNA testing. There might've been DNA samples missing, but that would've happened before they reached Volosin's lab."

"If you say so." Natalie stood up and stretched. "I'll let you go. You must be exhausted."

"Send me a quick text when you get back to the hotel."

"Why? Are you afraid I'll have another brake failure?"

"You never know."

Natalie ended the call and left the conference room. She sailed through the lobby and waved at Miles on her way out as he clicked the lock open for her. The parking lot had fewer cars than when she'd arrived.

As she made the short drive back to her hotel, the skies opened, and rain spattered against her car. She parked as close as she could to the hotel entrance and made a run for the lobby, holding her bag over her head.

The front desk clerk called to her as she made a beeline to the elevator.

"Ms. Brunetti, you have a message."

A message? She glanced at her phone clutched in her hand. Had Michael tried to reach her on her cell phone? Nope. Battery fully charged, no messages.

She shifted course and veered toward the front desk. "A telephone message?"

"It's actually a written note, or at least something in an envelope. Somebody left it on the counter earlier this evening." He handed her a small white envelope with her name written on it in a childish scrawl.

Something about that handwriting made her skin tingle, and she took the envelope with a trembling hand. Inserting her thumb between the flap and the envelope, she ripped it open.

She plucked out the folded sheet of paper and read the words.

Nat, meet me in our regular spot tonight.
Luv ya, Katie.

The *i* in Katie's name had a heart for the dot, just like Katie used to write it. The words blurred together, and she gripped the edge of the counter.

"Is everything okay, Ms. Brunetti?" The front desk clerk's face crumpled with worry.

Pinching the note between two fingers, she held it up. "Who left this?"

"I'm sorry. I don't know. It was sitting on the counter when I started my shift at five. I recognized your name and put it by my computer, so I wouldn't forget it when you walked in." His gaze darted to the envelope. "Is there a problem?"

"No, but I'd really like to know who left this. You must have cameras in here. Can I look at the footage?" Even she could recognize her hysterical tone, and the clerk's eyebrows were climbing higher and higher on his forehead.

"Ma'am, I'm sorry, but we can't allow guests to view our security footage. If there was a crime committed, if someone threatened you, we can get the police involved. They can request the footage."

"N-no crime. Just a note from…an old friend. I wanted to see if it was really her."

"If anything changes, ma'am, I'll be happy to get the police involved." He held up one finger. "And you can ask our day clerk, Daria. I believe she's working tomorrow."

"Thanks—" her gaze dropped to his nametag "—Ben. Maybe I'll talk to Daria."

Ben pasted the smile back on his face. "I'll give her a heads-up."

Natalie nodded and walked to the couch in the lobby on shaky legs. This had to be some kind of cruel joke. Had Zane done this? Did he really blame her for Katie's disappearance? Who else knew her identity? Did Dr. Volosin put two and two together. He was here at the lab when Katie disappeared. Would he have remembered the scared teen who'd narrowly escaped a similar fate that night?

She flattened out the note on her knee. She knew where their regular spot was. She'd been there earlier in the week. A swing set and slide sat at the entrance to the campsite near Devil's Edge Trail. She and Katie used to meet on the swings or up the stairs at the top of the slide. They'd even scratched their names into the metal of the slide.

Tonight. Someone wanted to meet her there tonight. Who knew about that meeting place? Who knew Katie put a heart over the *i* in her name? Had Katie returned? Maybe she had been a runaway all this time.

She wouldn't go alone. Not this time. Not that place.

She tapped Michael's number, and he picked up after the first ring. "You didn't have to call. Just a text, but I'm happy to hear your voice again."

And she was happy to hear his voice. The low, firm timbre made her feel grounded. "When I got back to the hotel, the clerk had a note for me at the reception desk. It was a note from Katie telling me to meet her in our regular spot tonight. Handwriting looked like hers, including a particular quirk."

"Someone's playing a prank on you, Natalie. Could it be Katie's teenage boyfriend?"

"Zane? I thought about that, but doesn't seem to be his style. He came right to the hotel to talk to me face-to-face. Someone else must know my identity, Michael."

"Where is this meeting spot?"

"Entrance to the Devil's Edge campsite—the playground equipment."

He sucked in a breath. "You're not considering it, are you?"

"I am if you come with me. Even if it's a prankster, I want to know who it is and why he's doing this."

"Okay, I'm closer to Devil's Edge than you are. Drive to my place and we'll go over in my car."

"Whoever wrote that note is not going to be there if I come with backup. You need to stay out of sight."

He growled. "I'll stay out of sight, but you'd better be strapped."

"Don't worry about that." She pushed up from the couch. "Separate cars. We come in the same way as the night we met. I'll park in the lot for the campsite, and you park in the pull-out for the trail and come in that way."

"Give me a head start. I want to be on that trail by the time you reach the parking lot. Hopefully, this rain will let up. That trail is nasty when it's wet."

"You leave now." She strode toward the elevator. "I'll go up and change clothes."

Fifteen minutes later, she'd changed into dark jeans, a black jacket and hiking boots. She texted Michael to make sure he was already on his way, and then she hopped in her car.

Before the turnoff for the campsite parking lot, Michael texted that he was at the trailhead and ready to go. Natalie's shoes scrunched over the soupy gravel of the parking lot, its one light trying valiantly to illuminate every corner. It failed.

Natalie's gaze swept the empty parking lot through the windshield wipers sluicing rain from her windshield in a rhythmic pattern that seemed to say "go back, go back."

But she wasn't a foolish teenager this time. She'd failed Katie before, but she wouldn't allow that to happen again. She flicked up the hood of her jacket and placed one booted foot on the ground, then grabbed a flashlight and patted her weapon in her pocket.

She had no intention of creeping around like a scared rabbit. She called out in a loud voice. "Hello? Who's out there? What kind of game are you playing?"

Drops of rain trickled from the edge of her hood and sprinkled her face. The chain on one of the swings whined, and she jerked her head around. A light breeze ruffled the tips of the leaves and pushed at the swing again, as if there was a phantom person sitting in it.

Katie used to love the swings.

Despite herself, Natalie whispered her friend's name.

Then she stamped her feet and shook the rain off her jacket. This person wanted to get under

her skin, wanted her to feel uneasy. They'd suc-
ceeded.

"Hello! You wanted this meeting. You got it."
Could Michael hear her inane yelling? She sure
as hell hoped so.

As she passed the swing set, she grabbed the
chain on one swing, pulled it back and released
it, sending the seat dancing back and forth. She
marched to the slide and grabbed the slippery
handrail. The metal steps clanged with each
tread to the top of the slide. The familiar covered platform beckoned, and she ducked to take
a seat in the space, which was big enough for
two to huddle within its confines.

Lowering her body, she leaned her back
against one rounded side. She flicked her flashlight over the graffiti and scratches on the inside
of the cover until she found the names—Katie
and Nat. Only Katie's name was scratched out.

A breath hitched in Natalie's throat and as she
reached out to trace the names, flakes of paint
came off on her fingertips. As she let out a stifled sob, a loud clang reverberated in the small
space, deafening her.

The next pop sounded more familiar. Someone was shooting at her.

Chapter Sixteen

Michael slogged into a puddle and swore. What did Natalie hope to find out here? At least she hadn't run out helter-skelter on her own. She'd called him. She trusted him. It had been a long time since someone trusted him.

He heard a woman yelling, and he froze. Was she in trouble already? Then he made out the words and realized Natalie was just announcing her presence. That was probably the best way to go about this. No sense sneaking up on someone.

An animal crackled in the bushes to his right, and he aimed his flashlight in the direction of the noise. It scurried away, and he continued on the trail. The rain-soaked earth gave off a loamy smell that he tasted in the back of his throat.

A branch cracked ahead of him. Startled, he tripped over a root. As he grumbled and clambered to his feet, the sound of gunfire echoed through the forest—and he knew hunting wasn't allowed in this area.

Before he was even steady, another shot rang out. He yelled, "Natalie."

His legs pumped like pistons as he ran through the woods, wet branches smacking his face, twigs grabbing at his hair. The shooting had stopped, and he hoped that at least one of those bullets had come from Natalie's weapon.

He stumbled into the campsite parking lot, Natalie's car taking up the space beneath the only light. He called her name again as he careened toward the playground equipment. One swing shivered as he blew past it, his flashlight scanning the old metal slide.

His eyes widened as he spotted Natalie flying down the slide on her back, her gun in front of her. She hit the ground and got into a crouch.

Michael called out quickly. "It's me. Michael."

"Get down, Michael. Someone just took a couple of shots at me, and I have no idea from which direction."

He dropped to the ground, but all he wanted was to get to Natalie. He army-crawled toward her, his elbows digging into the mud. When he reached her, she pulled him beneath the slide with her.

"Are you alright? Did you get hit?" He grabbed her shoulders and ran his hands down her arms.

"I'm fine. I was up on the slide's platform. It saved me. The first bullet hit the cover, but it didn't penetrate."

"And the second?" He fumbled for the phone in his jacket pocket.

"Missed the slide completely." She put her hand on his phone. "What are you doing?"

"I'm calling nine-one-one. Someone just shot at you."

"And what were you doing at Devil's Edge campsite in the middle of the night in the rain, Agent Brunetti. Well, you see I got a note from my best friend who went missing, presumed dead, thirteen years ago, and I thought we'd catch up on old times." She shook her head, and droplets from her hood sprinkled his face. "We can't call the sheriffs, Michael, just like I can't tell Detective Ibarra about the pendant found on Sierra's body. I'll blow my cover. If the FBI takes me off this audit, I'll never find out what happened to Katie, and you may never find out what happened to Raine. Nobody wants answers to these questions more than we do. Please."

She'd gripped his wrist in a vise hold, her gaze still turned outward, scanning the parking lot and the trees beyond. How far was she willing to take this? Someone tampered with her brakes and just took a couple of potshots at her. What next? How guilty did she have to feel about Katie's disappearance to risk her own safety?

The raindrops slowed to an intermittent pinging against the metal of the slide, and Michael's heartbeat matched the rhythm. If they called the cops, he'd have his own explaining to do as to why he was on the trail where his wife had been murdered.

He dropped his phone back in his pocket. "Let's get out of here. That bullet that hit the canopy of the slide, do you think we can find the pieces?"

"If it shattered, which is most certainly did, what good will that do us?"

"You work in forensics. If the pieces are big enough or there are enough of them, there's some reconstruction work that can be done. Also, you're lucky." He knocked on the side of the slide. "The slide is metal, but it's not that heavy. A different type of bullet may have even pierced it. A full-metal-jacket bullet probably wouldn't disintegrate at all. It's worth a look."

"Yeah, as long as someone's not shooting at us while we try to find it." She narrowed her eyes as she stared into the darkness.

"You're the one with the gun. Cover me while I take a look."

She dropped her chin to her chest. "Go."

He crawled toward the slide's ladder, leaving his flashlight behind. No sense in giving the shooter a target. When he got to the base of the slide, he cupped his hand around his phone and used the light to illuminate the ground.

He felt along the ground, his fingers becoming accustomed to the feel of the rocks and gravel that pebbled beneath them. He didn't expect the bullet or any fragments to still be hot. They'd been fired long enough ago to have cooled down, and the rain would've done its job, too.

His fingers stumbled across a smooth arc with a jagged edge, and he dragged his phone's light along the ground to highlight the piece. Definitely a bullet fragment.

His next find had his heart thumping—the distorted and flattened point of a bullet. He closed his hand around the bullet fragments and scuffed along the ground back to Natalie, her gun aimed in front of her as she scanned the area.

"I found something that might be useful." He unfurled his hand, the pieces stark against his palm. "This guy just made the biggest mistake of his life."

FOR ABOUT THE one hundredth time that night, Natalie thanked God that she'd had the good sense to call Michael before going on this fool's errand.

Hunched over, they ran back to Natalie's car, and she gunned it out of the parking lot. Michael had to point out his vehicle parked in the outlet, and she eased behind it, both cars hidden by overhanging tree branches and dripping leaves.

She cut the engine and sat with her eyes closed, breathing heavily. "I suppose that means the note wasn't from Katie."

"Unless Katie turned into a psychopath and doesn't want to be found." He rubbed her thigh through her damp and dirty jeans. "Someone wrote that note to lure you out to the campsite. But then you already knew that."

"I knew it, but—" she swung around to face him, tears hanging from her eyelashes "—when I was up on that slide, and I saw our names scratched into the metal, I remembered. And those memories hurt."

She blinked and a tear rolled down her cheek. Michael reached over and caught on his fingertip before it dripped off her chin.

His voice husky, he whispered in her ear. "It's not your fault. None of it is your fault."

Grabbing his hand, she pulled it to her lips and planted a kiss on the center of his palm, where he'd cupped the bullet that almost hit her. "Thank you for being there. Thank you for keeping my confidences when the information we have would probably clear your name in your wife's murder once and for all."

He wedged a finger beneath her chin. "I'm no saint. I have my own reasons for playing this close to the vest."

"Don't do that." She brushed a lock of wet

hair from his forehead. "Don't downplay your kindness, your integrity. You're one of the good guys, Michael Wilder."

A short and bitter laugh erupted from his lips. "I haven't been called a good guy in a long time. I tried to prevent a mother from seeing her child. I pushed her away instead of getting help for her. I left her on her own, and someone murdered her."

She placed two fingers against his soft lips. "What did you just tell me? It's not your fault. Stop blaming yourself for what had to be done to protect your daughter."

He puckered his lips against her fingertips. "How do you see me? How do you know me so well?"

"Because when I look at you, I see a reflection of all my doubts and fears…and my hopes. Because I still have hope, even more now that I've met you."

He reached for her across the seat, and she went willingly, squeezing past the steering wheel to straddle him in the passenger seat. His hand scooped through her curly mop of damp hair as he leveled her head with his for a kiss.

As his tongue probed her mouth, she ran her hands down his body and peeled off his jacket. Despite the cool temperatures, Michael wore a thin, white T-shirt beneath the jacket, and it clung to his muscled framed.

Her fingers danced beneath the hem of his shirt, and she lightly ran her nails across his chest. He shivered beneath her, encircling her waist with his hands. As she rocked against him, he lifted his hips and reached down to fumble with the fly of his jeans.

She shooed away his clumsy hands and deftly undid the button and zipper. He returned the favor. As she rose to her knees, he yanked her jeans and panties down her thighs.

Falling against him, they met, skin on skin, and a deep need pulsed in her core. She trailed her lips across the dark shadow of bristles on his chin and whispered in his ear, "Are we mad?"

"I've ached for you for days. When I heard the gunshots tonight, I felt a dread so pure, I couldn't name it." He smoothed her hair back from her face. "I can't name this."

"We don't need to label it." She shifted against him, feeling his physical need for her, fueling her desire for him.

He cupped her backside with his strong hands and lowered her hips until he entered her tentatively at first, and then his pelvis thrust forward. He slid deep inside her, filling every recess of longing and hurt.

She undulated against him until they found a cadence all their own, where he seemed to anticipate her desires, and she answered his every request. Their passion raged to a fever pitch, and Natalie threw out a hand against the foggy window to try for some leverage against the coming inferno.

When Michael came, he wrapped his arms around her waist and took her along for the ride. Throwing back her head, she pressed against him, gritting her teeth, her muscles taut, until she shattered.

They clasped each other close, arms, legs, clothes, all in a tangle, rocking together, not wanting to let the other go. Her head dropped to his shoulder, and her tongue darted out to lick his neck, salty with his sweat.

As she began to peel herself from his chest, a siren whooped twice, and a red light illuminated their love nest.

Wide-eyed, their gazes locked until Michael broke the spell by cursing. Natalie scrambled back into her seat, pulling at her jeans. Just as she grabbed her zipper, a hard object tapped at her window.

She murmured to Michael. "Are you decent?"

He grunted. "Getting there."

Natalie pulled her hair from her face and powered down the window to reveal Deputy Reynolds's grinning visage. Knots formed in her gut, as she searched his face for signs of recognition. She had darkness on her side.

His gaze jumped from her to Michael, and his mouth turned into an *O* and his eyebrows shot up and disappeared beneath his hat.

"Well, well. Is this a work meeting?"

The sight of his face made Natalie's stomach turn, but he didn't seem to know her beyond her purpose here in town. How could Katie have ever thought this smarmy loser was cute?

Michael's voice, so different from his whispers minutes before, boomed in the car. "Yeah. Yeah, it is. Are we breaking any laws, Deputy Reynolds?"

"Excuse me." He lifted his shoulders. "Saw the car, the steamy windows and figured you two were a couple of kids making out."

Tipping up her chin, Natalie huffed. "Clearly, we're not."

"Clearly." Reynolds's gaze dropped to her lap, where her jeans still gaped open. He rapped on the outside of the car with his knuckles. "Can't get enough of this area, hey, Wilder?"

Michael slicked back his hair with one hand. "Actually, Raine's homicide might have something to do with some cold cases—a few you even worked on, Reynolds."

Reynolds's face seemed to blanch in the darkness, but that could've been Natalie's imagination. His Adam's apple did bob. "Is that so?"

"Yep. Just discovered some bombshell evidence tonight…but you'll have to wait until tomorrow when I present it to Detective Ibarra. Now, if you're all done harassing us, we've got a meeting to finish up."

Reynolds backed away from the car, hands raised. "Carry on."

They sat still until they heard his car pull away. Then Natalie covered her mouth and giggled. Michael slapped his knee and let out a guffaw. They turned to each other at the same time and fell into each other's arms, laughing.

Natalie buried her face against Michael's T-shirt, wiping her tears. Maybe they laughed all the more because they knew tomorrow they'd be unleashing a firestorm.

Chapter Seventeen

The following morning, Natalie climbed into Michael's car, which was parked behind the lab. They'd both shown up for work but had kept their distance. She didn't know if she could look at him in public after what had happened the night before—and and not because of the shooting.

She'd rewound their encounter so many times last night, she'd had trouble sleeping. After Reynolds left and they'd had their giggling fit, they'd kept it all business, discussing the plan forward today. Then he'd given her a chaste kiss, gotten in his car and followed her back to the hotel…but not to continue what they'd started in the car. He just wanted to make sure she got back safely, which was almost as sexy as the sex.

She smoothed her wool skirt against her thighs and pulled the shoulder strap across her body. "I hope Reynolds isn't at the station."

"You said you didn't think he recognized

you." Michael started the engine and pulled out of the lab parking lot.

"I don't think he did, but in the light of day with me standing right in front of him instead of cowering in a car, he just might."

He snorted. "Didn't look like you were cowering to me. Are you ready for this?" He squeezed her knee right above her black boots. "Are you ready for the derision and disbelief as we lay out this story?"

"I'm ready if you are." She flipped down the visor and touched up her lipstick in the mirror. "Did you take care of the bullet fragments?"

"I put a rush on it. My friend at the Seattle lab owes me, so he'll keep quiet about it. We do each other favors sometimes."

She covered her ears. "I didn't hear that. It's exactly the type of thing we're supposed to un-cover."

"You're the one who wanted to keep the shooting quiet. I'm just helping you out."

"And I appreciate it. Does your contact in Se-attle think he can trace the bullet, even though it's in pieces?"

"He's done more with less. If he can detect the striations on the bullet and if anything matches in the database, we can trace it. Without bullets from the same gun or the firearm itself, we're out of luck." Michael brushed his knuckle across her cheek. "Any regrets about last night?"

Her skin prickled. "Besides getting shot at? No, it was great."

Chuckling, he pinched her chin. "That's not what I was talking about."

"The only regret I have—" she caught his hand and kissed the inside of his wrist "—is that we got interrupted. You?"

"Only that such a momentous event took place in a car. You deserve scented bath water and rose petals and champagne." He made a flourish with his hand.

"All that's nice, but doing it in a car is kinda hot."

And talking about it was even hotter. She changed the subject. "You know, I noticed something last night while I was on the slide that slipped my mind after…everything else."

"What was it?"

"Katie and I had scratched our names into the metal on the inside of the slide's canopy. Our names were still there, but someone had scratched out Katie's name. When I ran my fingers across the etching of her name, paint flakes came loose. It was as if someone had just scratched out the name recently. Do you think someone was on that platform before I came? Maybe he was waiting for me there first."

"If so, I'm glad he left. He would've had a clear shot at you walking up the ladder. That covering saved your life."

She'd thought the same thing. Actually, she'd thought it was Katie looking out for her, but she didn't want to admit that—not even to Michael.

Michael pulled into the parking lot of the sheriff's station, and the knots in Natalie's stomach tightened. Nothing much had changed about the building since she'd walked through those doors as a teenager with her parents, their faces stoic. She never would've believed she'd be back here as an adult, still with no answers about what happened to Katie that night.

Michael cupped her elbow up as they walked to the front doors, and then dropped it as he ushered her inside, ahead of him.

The deputy at the front desk greeted Michael, said hello to Natalie and then buzzed Detective Ibarra.

Detective Ibarra came out with a swagger to his walk and crinkles around his warm, dark eyes. If he'd been investigating Katie's murder, Natalie would've spilled her guts to him.

"Michael, good to see you again." The men shook hands, and then Ibarra turned his attention to her. "Michael doesn't even need to introduce you. Even if it weren't for the town buzz, I'd have you pegged."

Natalie's eyes widened, and she held her breath.

"Special Agent Natalie Brunetti, the Fed who came to town to straighten us out." Ibarra's broad grin took the irony out of his words, and his warm grasp put a nail in it.

"A bit of an exaggeration, Detective Ibarra, but I'll do my best to clarify some of the evidence in those old cases." She squeezed the large hand that engulfed hers.

He tilted his head. "But you two aren't here about an old case, are you?"

Michael answered. "Yes and no."

Ibarra invited them to his office in the back, and they settled in two comfortable chairs across from his desk. At least he hadn't put them in an interrogation room.

Ibarra flattened his tie against his shirt and folded his hands on his stomach. "What news do you have for me, Michael?"

"The dog came back home last night."

The pleasant smile on Ibarra's face dropped, and he hunched forward. "The dog that was with your wife when she was murdered?"

"That's right. She wandered into the backyard last night, a little worse for wear, but healthy."

"My God. If dogs could talk, huh? I'm assuming the dog didn't have any evidence on her—bloodstains, fibers, hair? After six months, that would've all washed away.

"There *was* evidence, Gil, just not the evidence you'd expect." Michael reached into his jacket pocket and pulled out Alma's bracelet, which he'd placed in a plastic bag. "This jewelry was wrapped around her collar."

Ibarra held out his hand. "Was it Raine's?"

Pulling out her phone, Natalie said, "No. We believe the bracelet belonged to a young murder victim from twelve years ago—Alma Nguyen, and I have Mrs. Nguyen's verification."

"What are you saying?" Ibarra brought the baggie close to his face, studying the bracelet within. "Alma's killer stole her bracelet and had it with him when he murdered Raine twelve years later?"

"And it's not the first time he's done it, Gil." Michael launched into everything they'd discovered and suspected about the jewelry of the dead women, giving Natalie ample opportunity to contribute, even though she still kept her true identity a secret.

When they'd finished, Ibarra didn't throw them out of his office, which was the good news. The bad? He narrowed his eyes, all warmth vanquished, replaced by cold, hard suspicion. The look he must get when listening to a suspect lying, knowing he has the receipts.

"First—" Ibarra held up one finger, nail bitten down to the quick "—why did a serial killer come out of retirement after twelve years to murder a woman a good ten years' senior to his usual victims?"

Michael interrupted. "Can I answer that before you get to number two?"

"Go ahead." Ibarra sounded bored, as if he knew what was coming.

"The killer could've been in prison, in a different area, been in different social circumstances like a marriage and children. As far as the age, this guy doesn't have a clear MO except for the jewelry. That's what links the victims."

"Michael—" Ibarra chewed on his lip "—if this guy killed Sierra and Alma and maybe Katie, his MO is victims in their late teens and early twenties. That's probably not gonna change for him. Was Raine a victim of opportunity for someone out of practice? Maybe. But you don't even have the jewelry part nailed down. An unfamiliar pendant was found with Sierra's body, but there's no way of knowing if that pendant belonged to Katie Fellows."

Natalie kept her eyes on Ibarra as she felt Michael's gaze hot on her cheek.

Ibarra sat forward in his chair, warming to his subject. "Sierra may or may not have been missing one of her many bangles. One of those bangles may have been on Alma's wrist, but we don't have a clear picture of it, and it's not listed in evidence. That's something for Agent Brunetti to expose in her report, I'm sure. That's sloppy police work. Sloppy forensics."

Natalie hit the desk with the flat of her hand, making both men jump. "And Alma's bracelet on Peaches?"

Picking up the corner of the baggie containing the bracelet and swinging it from his fingertips, Ibarra said, "I'll turn it over to the forensics lab in Seattle. They'll test it for blood, prints, DNA, the works. Of course, it's important, but is it Alma Nguyen's? You have a grieving mother ID'ing it from a texted picture on your phone twelve years after the fact."

"You're not going to reopen these cases or entertain the idea that Raine could've been the victim of a long-acting serial killer?" Michael slumped in his chair.

"I'm going to let Agent Brunetti do her job and let the chips fall where they may, even if it makes this department, and your lab, look bad. I'll support her in any way I can." He dropped the bracelet. "I'm also going to send someone out from Seattle to check on… Peaches, just in case, and as far as I'm concerned Michael, your alibi stands, and you're in no way a suspect in your wife's homicide."

Michael stood up abruptly. "You have to admit, Gil, the connections are interesting."

"If we had all the proof, I'd agree. These are cold cases. They're not closed. Maybe one day the proof will materialize."

As Michael held out his hand to Ibarra, he kicked the leg of Natalie's chair, and she jumped up. "Thanks for your time. Let me know when you want to examine the dog."

Ibarra shook Michael's hand. "I'm glad Peaches is back, Michael—for your little girl. I'm glad the dog is back home."

When they got back to the car, Natalie tipped back her head. "The worst part is that he's not wrong. We just don't have the proof."

"Proof would've been stronger if you'd told him what you know about Katie's pendant. Not pictures on a phone, not hearsay. It was your pendant, you let Katie wear it the night she disappeared, you saw it in the evidence from Sierra's homicide. Proof."

She whipped her head around at the hard edge to his voice. His tight jaw matched the tone. "If everyone knew about my connection to this area and to Katie Fellows, I wouldn't even be here. You never would've known the bracelet attached to Peaches belonged to a past homicide victim."

"But now we know the connections. It doesn't have to be you."

"Doesn't have to be me, what?" She pursed

her lips and dug her fingernails into the edge of the seat.

"You don't have to be the one to solve Katie's disappearance. You can help someone else do it. It's still justice."

Tears pricked the back of her eyes, and she swallowed. "Just take me back to the lab. I have work to do."

They finished the ride in silence and when Natalie got out of Michael's car, he stayed put. They'd already agreed they shouldn't be seen leaving together. She slammed the car door, anyway.

On a mission to get back to her office, she almost bumped into Jacob Reynolds moving some computer equipment. He made a grab for a keyboard as it slid from the cart. "Oops. Sorry, Agent Brunetti. Didn't see you."

She glared at his smiling face, so like his father's, and growled. "Watch where you're going."

When she closed the door to the conference room, she immediately felt bad. It wasn't Jacob's fault his father was a jerk. He seemed like a nice kid.

She hadn't seen Rachelle yet today and wondered if she was still sick. Should she go ahead and tour the DNA lab with Dr. Volosin alone? The thought made her skin crawl, and she pulled up the lab's personnel files. She found Rachelle's cell-phone number and called.

A woman answered tentatively after a few rings. "Rachelle? It's Natalie Brunetti. Are you still sick?"

"Not feeling great. I'm sorry I wasn't there for our appointment the other day, Natalie...and I know Dr. Volosin is back. He already called me with a thousand questions about how I ran the lab in his absence."

"I feel for you. I met him last night. Unpleasant." Natalie put her phone on speaker and strolled to the window to see if Michael had made his way back into the office yet. "I still need to tour the DNA lab. I wanted to wait until you're there, even if Dr. Volosin joins us."

"I'm still feeling under the weather, Natalie, and Dr. Volosin doesn't make me feel much better, but..."

"But what?" The quality of Rachelle's voice had changed. It had taken on a quality of urgency, one she'd heard the first time Rachelle suggested Natalie visit the lab before Volosin returned.

"I'd like to talk to you about a few things, and it would be better if we were away from the lab. C-can you come to my place this afternoon, or even after work?"

"I can do that. Are you far from the lab? I can drop by when I'm done at the lab, if that's okay."

"That's fine."

Rachelle gave her the address of her town house on the lake, and Natalie jotted it down on a pad of paper. After the call, Natalie tapped the pen against the pad. Rachelle hadn't even been working at the lab at the time of the cold cases Natalie was investigating. Were things still off here? Or did Rachelle have some information about her boss who was here at the time of the cold cases?

For the next several hours, Natalie put aside the distractions and her own investigative efforts to work on the cold cases assigned to her. The other victims deserved their justice as much as Katie did hers.

She finished up the day by sending her boss another report. He'd be happy with her progress, and she had to keep him happy to stay out here and complete *all* her work, even the stuff he didn't know about.

As she packed up her files and laptop, she glanced at her phone. Michael hadn't dropped by or contacted her the rest of the day. She could understand his frustration, but she had to do this her way, or not at all.

Before she left the office, she entered Rachelle's address in her phone's GPS. Maybe she should tell Michael about her off-site meeting with Rachelle, but if the woman had info about the lab's current state, maybe it would be better to keep this to herself.

The drive to Rachelle's place didn't take long and offered relaxing views of the lake on one side. These developments had gone up since her residence here in Marysville. She'd remembered her father complaining about the proposal to build on this side of the lake, but the tasteful town houses fit in with their surroundings.

Natalie wheeled into the guest parking lot and nabbed an empty spot. She had an easy time finding Rachelle's building as a backlight illuminated the numbers on each one. She'd parked close to Rachelle's building and the walkway that led into the courtyard.

Her boots clicked on the pavers, a harsh contrast to the soothing sounds of a bubbling fountain in the center of the courtyard. She ducked onto a rustic path that led to more town houses around the back.

Spotting Rachelle's address, Natalie took the gravel path next to the lakeside walking trail to the town house. Moving furniture into this place had to be hell, but she'd take the inconvenience for the bucolic beauty.

A row of neat flowers edged the porch, and Rachelle had added more splashes of color with adorable window boxes. Natalie rang the doorbell next to the red door.

She shifted from one foot to the other, giving Rachelle time. If she'd been the one home sick all day, it would take her a while to get to the front door. Several seconds later, Natalie pressed the doorbell again, this time putting her ear to the solid door to listen for the sound of the bell inside. Yep, it worked.

Natalie placed her hand flat against the door. Was she okay in there? Did Rachelle have the flu? Nobody ever said.

Natalie curled her hand into a fist and knocked. "Rachelle? It's Natalie. Are you alright?"

Was that a moan? A rustle? Natalie bit her bottom lip and tried the door. The handle turned beneath her fingers, and she pushed open the door.

She squealed as a cat jumped off a bookshelf and swished its tail with an angry squawk.

"Rachelle?" She closed the door behind her, so the cat wouldn't run outside, and crept into the town house, although she didn't know why she needed to be quiet. In fact, the quiet was unnerving.

She called Rachelle's name again. A lamp lit the living room, along with the muted TV, but most of the light came from the kitchen. The cat had gone that way, so Natalie followed it.

As she peered into the kitchen, she gasped. Rachelle was lying crumpled on the tile floor, a broken bowl beside her and a smear of blood on her face.

Chapter Eighteen

Michael stretched out on the floor and scratched Peaches's head. "You must have a story to tell."

Molly poked her head out of the kitchen. "Do you want any more food? I'm putting it away."

"No, I'm good."

"I thought you might bring Natalie back here for dinner, since we didn't get to feed her last night." She put a hand on her hip.

"Have you turned into Mom? Mind your own business." He lifted Peaches up and placed her on his stomach. "We need to fatten her up."

"Sorry Ivy went to sleep so soon after dinner. She was playing with Peaches all day. Wouldn't let her out of her sight."

"That's fine. She needs her sleep. I'll spend time with her this weekend." Michael's phone rang, and his heart skipped a beat when he saw his friend, Deputy Cole Foster, pop up on his display. Did they want to check out the dog already?

"What's up, Cole?"

"Just got a call on my radio. Thought you might wanna know. One of your lab employees was found dead in her home."

"What? Who?" Michael nudged Peaches from his stomach and staggered to his feet.

"It's Dr. Rachelle Butler. She works in the lab, right?"

"Rachelle? Cause of death? She's been out sick, but I had no idea she was dangerously ill."

"Can't tell you much more than that. The FBI agent you have working for you found her body."

Michael clamped the back of his neck. "In Rachelle's home? She was in Rachelle's home?"

"Dude, I don't have anything more than that. Just happened. I'm on my way."

"Address." Michael grabbed a pair of running shoes. "Do you have Rachelle's address?"

As soon as Cole recited the address to him, Michael ended the call and strode to the closet for his jacket. "Molly, I have to go out."

Before she could answer, he slammed the door. How was Rachelle dead, and what was Natalie doing in the middle of it?

He drove faster than the speed limit to reach Rachelle's place, the new development out by the lake. Rachelle was a doctor. She should've known if she needed medical attention. Hell, she hadn't even looked that sick the day she came to tell him she was leaving early.

Emergency vehicles clogged the parking lot, so Michael pulled onto the street outside the town-house development. He didn't need the address number to find Rachelle's place. As he walked up to the building, he could see a deputy questioning a tearful Natalie off to the side.

Recognizing him, the deputy keeping the lookie-loos at bay allowed Michael to dip beneath the yellow tape. CSIs were already on the scene, but his lab wouldn't be getting the evidence. Were they there out of courtesy for Rachelle, or did they believe her death was something other than natural or accidental?

As Deputy Ellis walked past, Michael grabbed his arm. "What happened in there? How did Rachelle die?"

Ellis shrugged. "We don't know that yet. The only visible injury she sustained was a cut to her cheek, but that was from a broken bowl. Looks like she fell to the floor with the bowl in her hand or on the counter, it broke, and a piece cut her face."

Michael pinched the bridge of his nose. "Did she die from the fall? Head injury?"

"Not that we can tell, unless there's something internal. Uh—" Ellis glanced over his shoulder "—her skin was blueish, and she had a little vomit in her mouth."

"Well, she didn't do drugs. Maybe she took

something for her illness. She'd called in sick, but she didn't tell me what was wrong."

Grabbing Michael's shoulder, Ellis said, "We owe it to one of our own to figure out what happened."

"Do you know what Agent Brunetti was doing here?"

"Ask her yourself." Ellis jerked his head to the right at Natalie approaching them, still wearing her knee-high boots from this morning, her hands shoved into her pockets.

Ellis asked, "Are you doing okay?"

Natalie waved him off and grabbed Michael's sleeve. "Did he tell you what happened?"

"Just that you found her on the floor. A piece of glass from a broken bowl cut her face but no other injuries." He wanted to pull her into his arms, but it wasn't the time or the place. "Do you want to tell me what you were doing at Rachelle's place after hours?"

"Not here." She strode back to the deputy who was questioning her earlier and had a brief discussion with him. Then she made her way back to him, stumbling when the coroner's van pulled up.

When she reached his side, she prodded him in the back. "They're done with me. Let's talk in my car."

He followed her to the rental and slid into the

passenger seat. "What the hell is going on, Natalie?"

"I didn't tell you before, but Rachelle wanted to show me around the DNA lab before Dr. Volosin returned."

"Doesn't surprise me. He's a difficult guy to work with." He rapped his knuckle against the window. "Can you drive out of this parking lot? I'm in the street."

Natalie started the car and maneuvered around the emergency vehicles to get to the street in the front. She pulled behind his car and cut the engine. "Anyway, Rachelle got sick, and Volosin returned from his trip, which meant he'd be present during my tour of the lab. So I called Rachelle at home today to ask her if she wanted to be present during my lab review. She got all weird and told me she needed to see me, that she had something to tell me."

Michael rubbed his eyes, suddenly so tired. "Did she give you any hints?"

"None, but she definitely wanted to have this conversation away from the lab."

A pain stabbed him at the base of his neck. "What are you suggesting? She didn't feel safe at the lab? She thought something was going on there?"

"Whoa." Natalie cut her hands through the air. "I'm not suggesting anything. I'm telling you what she said. You're the one who doesn't trust me."

Michael toyed with the scrap of paper in his pocket. "How did she sound on the phone? Ill? Did she ever mention what illness she had?"

"She didn't say, and I didn't ask. But she didn't sound congested, and she didn't seem worried about being contagious. Maybe she wasn't sick. Maybe she didn't want to be there when Dr. Volosin returned."

"If she wasn't sick, how did she die? Did her fall look serious to you? Could there have been something she hit her head on when she fell?"

Natalie sniffed and dabbed the tip of her nose. "I don't know. I felt for a pulse, tried CPR. Her body felt cool but not cold, which would make sense, as I spoke to her on the phone several hours before I found her body. Michael, I think someone murdered Rachelle."

Pressing the heel of his hand against his forehead, he said, "What could she possibly know about any of this? Did you talk to her about the jewelry we found and the other connections?"

"Of course not." She shifted in her seat impatiently. "But she was about to tell me something about the lab. Something she didn't want anyone else there to hear."

Michael ground his back teeth together, sick of veiled accusations against him and the forensics lab he ran. He pulled the balled-up piece of paper from his pocket and bobbled it on his palm in front of Natalie.

"What's this?" She pinched the paper between her fingers and plucked it from his hand.

"While you were looking for dirt on the lab, I was busy trying to find out who shot at you last night."

"You got a match?" With trembling fingers, she picked open the crumpled piece of paper. "John Westfall, Shady View Rest Home in Everett? This is the shooter?"

"One fragment of the bullet was large enough to contain striations. My friend in Seattle was able to pick them up and run them through his database. Something finally went our way. He was able to match it to an old forty-five-caliber Beretta."

"Used in the commission of a crime? How could it still be on the street?" Natalie flattened the wrinkled scrap of paper to her chest, as if they'd found the Holy Grail.

"Wouldn't exactly call it the crime of the century. Some old guy was causing a nuisance, drunk and shooting at targets in the forest."

"John Westfall."

"Right. Deputies picked him up, checked his gun—the Beretta, registered to him—and let him off with a warning. They did put the bullets in the National Integrated Ballistic Information Network, though."

"NIBIN. Of course, I know it." She blew out a breath that fluttered the edges of the paper. "And the bullets from last night matched the bullets from this Beretta."

"Correct."

"Then what are we waiting for? Let's take a trip to the Shady View Rest Home."

NATALIE SAILED OUT of the hotel with cups of coffee in each hand and placed one on the hood of Michael's car as she opened the passenger door. He'd closed the forensics lab today in honor of Rachelle's death the day before. Nobody would've been able to get anything done, anyway.

"Thought you might want a coffee for the drive to Everett. Black?" She put the paper cup in the cupholder for him.

"Thanks. If you can dump one of those little creamers in there, that'd be great. If not, don't worry about it." He started the car. "It's just a thirty-minute drive, on the outskirts of Everett."

"I can manage the cream if you idle for a second while I pour it in." She peeled back the foil on the creamer and tipped it into Michael's coffee. She swirled the liquid with a stir stick and placed the cup back in the holder. "I didn't tell you. The FBI ordered the rental-car company to do a more thorough examination of the brakes and send them the report."

"Are they concerned that someone may have tampered with the rental car belonging to one of their agents?"

"That's why they're ordering additional tests." She sipped her own coffee. "Did the cops send someone to look at Peaches yet?"

"Nope. I'm getting the feeling that they think I'm some kind of jinx."

"Maybe we can get something on this John Westfall. Were you able to find out anything more about him besides his current residency at Shady View?" Natalie hadn't had any time of her own to check into him after leaving Rachelle's last night. The car accident, the shooting and discovering Rachelle had taken a toll on her body and mind. She'd fallen into bed last night and had slipped into an exhausted sleep. The old nightmare didn't even revisit her.

"Not much. Enlisted in the navy. Worked at Boeing for years, and retired from there when he had his accident."

"The shooting accident?"

Michael shook his head. "No, he almost drowned. Suffered brain damage. That's why he's in the rest home. He's not that old, or at least not as old as you'd expect a resident of Shady View to be."

"Brain damage, huh?" Natalie swirled her coffee and watched the little whirlpool in the cup. "Is he going to be able to talk to us?"

"No clue." Michael lifted his shoulders. "But it probably means he didn't sneak out of the rest home and murder Raine or fix your brakes or shoot at you."

Natalie folded her hands in her lap and tried to squeeze away the disappointment she felt. When Michael had told her about the bullets matching Westfall's gun, she'd figured they'd finally gotten a break. Something going their way for once. Now, the prospect of an interview with Westfall didn't seem so promising.

They arrived at Shady View faster than Natalie had time to regain her previous optimism. She eyed the spruce, the firs, the maples and alders ringing the property, blocking out the daylight. "They weren't kidding about the shady view, were they?"

"Shady and green."

Michael got out of the vehicle, and she followed suit, inhaling the competing smells from the different trees that gradually melded into a fresh scent that slapped the face.

She shivered and zipped up her jacket. "This

is pretty, but I wouldn't want to end up in a place like this. Too dark."

"I know." Michael flipped up his collar. "I mean, they have a bay, a river and a sound out here. You'd think they could've given the guests a nice water view."

She jostled Michael's shoulder with her own as they approached the entrance. "They're not guests."

A smiling woman greeted them at the front desk. "Hello, I'm Monica. Welcome to Shady View. Are you looking for a place for your loved one?"

Michael spoke up first. "Uh, no. We came to visit one of your…guests. John Westfall."

Did Natalie imagine it, or did Monica's smile dim just a little?

"Do you have an appointment to see John?" Monica started clicking away on the keyboard in front of her.

"No. John's an old friend of my father's. I was in the area, and thought I'd drop in to say hello from my dad. That's alright, isn't it, Monica?"

Maybe Michael's blue eyes mesmerized her, but Monica was all smiles again. She even had a pink tinge to her cheeks. "Of course. We just need to ask John. What's the name?"

Natalie kicked Michael's foot. What if Westfall refused to see them?

"Tell him it's Jerry Wilder's son—from their old navy days."

"Just a moment, Mr. Wilder. I'll call his nurse."

As Monica got on the phone, Michael wandered to the window to look out on the unrelenting green.

Natalie came up behind him and whispered, "Is your dad's name Jerry?"

"No. Just thought I'd try a common name. Is he going to remember everyone he served with?"

"I don't know. These old guys can surprise you. My grandfather couldn't remember my nephew's name, but he could tell you all about the Battle of the Bulge…in detail."

"Great." Michael spun around when Monica called out.

"Mr. Wilder? John has agreed to your visit. Room one-sixty-five, down your hall, to the right."

"Thank you, Monica," he said sotto voce to Natalie as Monica buzzed the door. "We're in."

They ticked off the room numbers as they walked down the hallway, their shoes squeaking on the linoleum floor. Natalie's nose twitched at the smell of antiseptic that tried to cover the mustiness that seeped through. The denizens of Shady View should open the windows more and let in some of that fresh air.

When they reached 165, the door stood partially open, and Michael tapped on it before walking inside. The balding man facing them in a wheelchair did not look like he was capable of standing, never mind cutting brake lines and shooting a gun.

Undeterred, Michael pulled a chair close to Westfall, his knees almost touching those of the disabled man. "John, can you hear me?"

One side of John's mouth quirked upward in a permanent grin, but he nodded.

Michael got straight to the point. "John, did you own an old Beretta?"

John moved a stiff hand in his lap, the fingers curled inward. Natalie held her breath as she focused on his hand.

A nurse bustled into the room with a board under her arm. "If you expect to have a conversation with John, he needs his bell."

"Bell?" Natalie watched as the nurse put the board on John's lap and set a call bell on top of it, positioning his hand on top of the bell.

"One for yes, two for no. Right, John?" She squeezed John's shoulder and exited the room, leaving the door open.

Michael exchanged a look with Natalie and started again. "Did you own a Beretta, John?"

John's finger went to the ringer, which he tapped once.

"Do you still have that gun?"

Two rings.

"Was it stolen?"

Two rings.

Natalie held up a hand to Michael and asked, "Does a family member have the gun?"

Two rings.

Michael hunched forward, almost in Michael's face. "Do the cops have that gun?"

One ring.

Natalie gasped and drew back. "How could that gun be in police custody? They gave it back to him. It said so in the report, right?"

"Unless the cops gave the gun to a family member, and that relative didn't tell John he still had the gun." Michael rubbed a twitch at the corner of his eye.

"Is that what the report said?"

Michael sighed. "It didn't specify whether it was given back to John or a family member."

"Can I try something else?" Natalie put her hand on Michael's arm, and he drew back from John.

"John, did you know about a girl named Katie Fellows?"

One ring.

Natalie's adrenaline spiked, and she dropped to her knees in front of John. "Did you harm her? Did you, John?"

The other side of John's mouth lifted. His

crooked finger hovered over the ringer. Natalie's breath came in short spurts as she watched him lower his finger to the bell.

He pressed down.

She waited, heart pounding.

The finger stayed pinned against the ringer.

She lifted her gaze to his face, noticing for the first time the blackness of his eyes as he stared at her. Fury whipped through her veins. "Ring the bell, John. Yes or no. Ring it."

"Natalie." Michael stroked her back, but she shrugged him off.

"Ring the bell, you bastard. Ring it once. I know it was you."

"Mr. Wilder!" The nurse had come charging back into the room. "What is going on in here? Get out now, or I'll call the police."

Michael gripped her arm and practically dragged her to her feet. "Let's go Natalie. There was a misunderstanding. We're leaving now. John's fine."

The nurse crouched in front of John's wheelchair and as Michael led her from the room, Natalie craned her neck around the nurse's broad back to meet those black eyes again. Then she heard the bell ring once.

Chapter Nineteen

Natalie pulled out of Michael's grip. "Did you hear it, Michael? Did you hear the bell? He rang it twice. He's responsible for Katie's disappearance. I know it. He knows it."

"Shh." Michael took her by the shoulders and pinned her against the wall. "If that happened, if that's what your heard, we'll figure it out, but not like this."

She sagged, all the fight draining from her body. "*If* that happened? You don't believe me? You didn't hear the two rings?"

"I heard a very angry nurse ready to get us kicked out of here. How is that going to help?" He took her hand and kissed the inside of her wrist. "Let's not give them that opportunity."

Her head throbbed as the anger dissipated. Michael was right, but she knew in her heart that they had their man. He took Katie. He murdered Sierra and Alma. He stopped because he almost drowned and became disabled. Did he have a copycat now? Did the person who killed

Raine mimic John Westfall to throw the cops off the scent?

She allowed Michael to lead her outside, and the crisp air hitting her face did its job. Her head cleared. Her brain clicked back into focus.

"It's him, Michael. We have to tell the sheriff's department. They need to investigate him thoroughly."

They sat on a bench outside the facility, and he slung his arm across her shoulders. "They'll have a hard time questioning him."

She twisted her head to face him. "Is that supposed to be a joke?"

"It's not a joke, Natalie. It's the truth." His body stiffened. "Uh-oh."

"What's wrong?" She followed the nod of his head toward a sheriff's car pulling into the parking lot. "Oh. I'll take all the blame. Don't worry."

The patrol vehicle parked, and two deputies got out and walked toward them, their equipment clinking on their duty belts. Michael murmured, "I know both these guys. We got this."

One of the deputies tipped back his hat. "Michael? Did you already tell her?"

"Tell her?" Michael stood, resting his hand on Natalie's shoulder. "Tell who, what?"

Natalie pinned her hands between her knees. If she got arrested out here, she'd be in big trouble with the Bureau.

"Mrs. Butler?"

"Wait, who?" Michael placed a hand across his furrowed brow.

Natalie stood up beside him, swaying a little.

"Mrs. Butler. Rachelle's grandmother."

"Here?" Michael jerked his thumb over his shoulder at the entrance to Shady View.

"Oh, sorry, man. I thought you came here to notify Mrs. Butler about her granddaughter's death. Got my hopes up there for a minute that I wouldn't have to do it."

Natalie squeezed Michael's bicep, her fingernails digging into the material of his jacket. "Rachelle's grandmother is a resident of Shady View?"

The deputy dipped his head. "She is. She's Rachelle's closest relative in the area. They already called her parents in Atlanta, but her parents wanted someone to come out and tell the grandma."

"Sorry you guys have to deliver the bad news." He pinched Natalie's waist. "Any updates on what happened to Rachelle?"

"I'm hearing suicide, but that's just a rumor. I'm just telling you because...you know, you were her boss, and you're my friend." He put a finger to his lips. "You didn't hear it from me."

"No, no. Of course not. Appreciate it, man. We'll let you get to it."

Natalie walked beside Michael, afraid to talk, afraid to turn around. When they got into the car with the doors closed, Michael whistled. "What are the odds?"

"The odds that the man who owned the gun that shot at me two nights ago is in the same rest home as the grandmother of the woman who just turned up dead in her home after trying to tell me something? The odds of that being a coincidence are zero." She grabbed Michael's hand as he reached for the ignition button. "We have to go back in there and talk to Mrs. Butler. She must know Westfall, know what he is. She told Rachelle, and someone on the outside took care of her for Westfall."

"Stop, Natalie." He brushed aside her fingers and started the engine. "We cannot go back inside and grill an old woman who just lost her granddaughter. Your scenario makes no sense, anyway. I could understand why Mrs. Butler might be too afraid to tell anyone in authority about Westfall, although he doesn't look like much of a physical threat, but why would Rachelle keep that information to herself. If her grandmother told her something about Westfall, Rachelle would've gone straight to the police."

Falling back against the seat, Natalie covered her face with her hands. "I know you're right, but there's something just out of my reach. Some connection between Westfall and Mrs. Butler."

"And the lab." Michael clenched the steering wheel. "If what Rachelle had to tell you concerned only Shady View or John Westfall, why did she have to meet you at her house instead of the lab?"

"I wish I knew. Have there been any crimes at Shady View? Any evidence the lab has processed from there?"

"Not that I know of." Michael shook his cup, and the dregs of his coffee sloshed in the bottom. "Do you want to get something to eat on the way back to your hotel?"

"I'm not very hungry." As Natalie yawned, her phone rang. "It's my boss. He liked my report, but I haven't told him that I discovered a dead body." She answered the call. "Hey, boss."

"Brunetti, I want you on the first plane back to DC."

He must've heard about her involvement with Rachelle. "I can explain. Dr. Butler is the one who called me. I believed she had pertinent information about the lab and my cold cases."

He paused. "Who the hell is Dr. Butler?"

Natalie's mouth went dry, and she peeled her lips apart. "What are you talking about then? You were happy with my work yesterday. Why the sudden turn-around?"

"Yesterday, I didn't realize you were out there in Marysville under false pretenses, Nat Cooper. I don't know who you think you are pulling a stunt like that, but I'm suspending you as of now. We'll have an investigation when you get back."

"Give me chance to tell my side of the story." Natalie licked her lips and tried to keep her voice steady.

"You'll get your chance—at your disciplinary hearing."

"H-how…?"

"How did I find out?" he growled, which was never a good sign with Jefferson. "That's the kicker. Not only did you humiliate me and the Bureau, I had to find out from an anonymous source and then do the research myself to verify."

"I…" Jefferson had already ended the call before she could formulate an answer. She sat frozen, staring at the passing scenery, a green blur.

"What just happened?" Michael's voice sounded a million miles away.

She cranked her head to the side, and a muscle at the corner of her mouth danced wildly. "My boss found out about my connection to Katie Fellows…from an anonymous source."

"Somebody must've recognized you, but why rat you out to the FBI? Could it have been Reynolds?"

"It could've been Reynolds, but why would he want to remain anonymous? It also could've been someone who wanted all the evidence on the table. Someone who wants to connect Raine's homicide to the others even more than I do."

Michael's eyes widened. "Just a minute. First you accuse me of hiding things at the lab, and now you think I squealed on you to your boss?"

"You know what, Michael? Just take me back to the hotel." She folded her arms and clenched her teeth, more to hold back the sobs than in anger. "I'm done."

MICHAEL YANKED AT the front door of the lab, but it didn't budge. He pulled again in anger, almost wrenching his shoulder, before the lock buzzed and clicked. By the time he stepped foot in the lobby, he'd remembered that he was the one who had closed the lab for the day.

Sam was standing behind the security desk with a worried look on his face. "Sorry about that, Michael. When you ordered the office closed, I figured that meant locking up, even though a few people did come in to work."

"My fault." Michael fumbled for his badge in his pocket and flashed it at Sam. "Habit. Who's here?"

"Dr. Volosin, catching up. Nicole Meloan, cleaning up the evidence room for the inspection, and that kid Jacob is helping her." Sam cleared his throat. "Sorry to hear about Rachelle."

"Yeah, tragic." Michael stomped up the stairs, his feet like blocks of lead.

He left his door open as he collapsed behind his desk. After everything he and Natalie had been through this week, she still didn't believe he wasn't the anonymous source who had reported her.

He didn't want her to leave, ever. He'd wanted to make this right for her, to give her peace. But maybe now that everything was out in the open, that solution could be realized faster.

She could go to Ibarra now and tell him about that pendant. Someone had taken it from Katie and put it on Sierra. Those two cases were linked.

Could that old, wrecked man in the rest home really be responsible for the murders of three young women? And what did any of it have to do with Raine?

Natalie mentioned something outside Shady View. She'd said something about someone on the outside assisting Westfall. He hadn't been able to discover much about Westfall before heading out to the rest home to see him, but he did have two children. They must be adults. Were they still living in the area?

He logged in to his laptop and started checking databases. He wasn't part of the law enforcement branch of the Washington State Patrol and didn't have access to the same information as they did. He could probably circumvent protocol and get some info on the sly.

A shadow passed by the blinds of the windows that looked onto the rest of the office, and Michael glanced up. A door closed quietly down the hall. Volosin wouldn't be upstairs, unless he was going to the lunchroom, but if Jacob Reynolds was still in the office, he could be anywhere. He had access to most areas of the lab.

Michael had hired him as a favor to a friend of Reynolds, and the kid had proved himself to be competent, friendly and helpful. Maybe too helpful. He always seemed to be into everything, offering his services to everyone.

Michael got up from his desk and poked his head out the door. Dead quiet.

When he returned to his computer, he tried to find information about Westfall's two children. Nothing came up under that name in Marysville. He couldn't even find any property listed for Westfall. He needed the help of his buddies in the department. Or maybe once Natalie came clean about her identity and her connection to Katie, the sheriff's department would take this link to Westfall seriously and get some warrants.

In the meantime, Michael snapped his laptop

closed and jumped to his feet. He could at least try to find out who had visited Westfall at Shady View. If the man did have outside help, that assistant would have to visit Westfall in person. The man couldn't speak on the phone or send an email without help.

Michael packed up his stuff and jogged down the stairs, raising a hand to Sam as he exited the building. With any luck, Monica would not be working reception at Shady View. After Natalie's outburst this morning, he wouldn't make it two feet past Monica.

He drove back to Everett, barely noticing the scenery, his foot getting heavier on the accelerator. If he could make this right for Natalie maybe she'd trust him again. Maybe she'd stay.

He parked on the edge of the parking lot and slinked along the side of the building to peek in the window before heading through the front doors. He released a long breath when he spotted someone other than Monica sitting behind the reception desk.

Squaring his shoulders, he entered the lobby. Low-burning candles emitted a peachy scent that beat the hell out of the antiseptic burn in the hallways. His gaze darted to the doors that led to the rooms in the back. If that nurse from this morning came through those doors, he'd be toast.

He nodded briskly at the smiling woman behind the computer. She said hello without asking him if he had a loved one he wanted to park here. Good. He had a different image to project.

"Good afternoon, ma'am. I'm with the Washington State Patrol, and I need to have a look at your visitor log for the past few months." He placed a hand on his badge that did, in fact, have Washington State Patrol on it, but it didn't much look like law-enforcement ID, especially as the picture had him in a white lab coat.

Her kind face creased, and her lips turned down. "Oh, this must be in connection to poor Mrs. Butler's granddaughter. The police were out here this morning, I understand."

"Yes, we were here to notify Mrs. Butler. Now, something else has come up, and we need to check the visitor logs."

"Two months, you say?" The woman, Fay, was already clicking keys on her computer, and Michael stood still, his muscles tense.

Fay tapped the guest book on the counter. "We have people sign in here, but then we transfer that information to the computer for easier access. We do keep all the books, though, if you want to see those."

"I think just the names would suffice for now. The computer record includes the resident the visitor signed in to see, correct?"

"Oh, yes, so you'll see all of Mrs. Butler's visitors, although honestly, I think it was just her granddaughter, who was a sweet person and a doctor." Fay tapped a key with a flourish. "I'm printing the pages out for you now."

"Thank you, Fay. We appreciate your help." *More than you'll ever know.*

She whipped the pages from the printer and handed them to Michael. As he reached for them, she playfully pulled them back. "I even highlighted Mrs. Butler's name for you."

"You're so considerate." He turned just as the door to the hallway swung open. He didn't want to move to draw attention to himself, so he ducked his head to scan the pages in his hands.

"Barb isn't eating her meals. I'm going to see if she'll have some nutritional supplement."

Recognizing the nurse's voice from this morning, Michael buried his head even farther in the pages. He ran his finger down the list, searching for John Westfall's name. He found the first instance and dragged his finger to the right under the visitor name column.

He almost dropped the whole sheaf of papers on the floor. How was this possible? He found the Westfall entry, and the next and the next, and the same visitor name met his horrified gaze each time.

He stood with his back turned to the conversation, clutching the edges of the papers, a bead of sweat trailing down his temple to his ear. When the nurse went back through the door, Michael spun around to face Fay.

His finger jabbed at the name of Westfall's visitor. "Do you know John Westfall?"

Fay's mouth grimaced before she managed to turn it into a tight smile. "Yes, I know Mr. Westfall."

"This is his only visitor? Are you sure?"

Tilting her head, she said, "Of course, I'm sure. I thought you were looking at Mrs. Butler's visitors."

With his hands trembling, Michael dug his phone from his pocket and swiped through his photos until he found one from the office Christmas party last year. He used his fingers to zero in on one face in the group. "This? Is this his visitor?"

Fay put on a pair of glasses and leaned in. "Yes. That's Mr. Westfall's daughter, Nicole."

Chapter Twenty

Natalie put her eye to the peephole in her hotel-room door and peered at Nicole standing there with a basket in her hands, a hood over her head. She looked like Little Red Riding Hood, delivering goodies to Grandma.

She opened the door. "Hi, Nicole. C'mon in."

As Nicole stepped through the door, she shook the hood back off her head. "It's starting to sprinkle outside."

"I know. I was going to take a walk and get some fresh air. I feel cooped up in here." Natalie waved her hand behind her at the room. She hadn't started packing yet. Hadn't even booked a flight home. Since she was suspended, she might as well take her time.

She sniffed the air. "Whatever you have in that basket smells great."

"Scones." Nicole lifted the cloth napkin covering the contents of the basket. "I baked some scones and thought I'd bring some to you. I'm so sorry you discovered Rachelle yesterday. So heartbreaking."

"It was devasting. I'm glad Michael closed the office today. Not sure anyone would get any work done." She declined to mention to Nicole that she wouldn't be returning to the lab…ever.

Nicole placed the basket on the credenza next to the TV. "Do you have any tea in here? We can have ourselves some afternoon tea and scones."

Natalie snatched up the tin next to the electric pot. "Earl Grey?"

"Perfect." Nicole held out the basket. "Help yourself."

Natalie's stomach rumbled as she smelled the sweet buttery goodness of the scones, remembering she'd refused Michael's invitation to lunch. She should call him. She spoke out of anger. There's no way Michael would've betrayed her like that.

She picked up a corner of one of the scones with her fingers and bit into the crusty edge, her teeth sinking into the softer center. She brushed the crumbs from her chin. "These are perfect."

"I told you. I can't cook, but baking's my thing." Nicole turned her back on Natalie to rip open the tea bags and drop them into the hotel's paper cups. "Have you heard anything from Michael about the cause of Rachelle's death? I mean, I know she went home sick, but I thought she just had an upset stomach."

"Oh, really? That's what it was?" Natalie broke off another piece of scone and stuffed it in her mouth. "Haven't heard a word from Michael. He and I…"

"You two had a disagreement?" The kettle beeped, and Nicole lifted it from the base to pour the boiling water over the tea bags. "He does have anger-management issues, but you two seemed so…close."

Natalie swallowed one bite and went right in for another to avoid talking about Michael with Nicole. Anger management? She could see it. The man was practically seething when she first met him.

Nicole held out a cup. "Cream or sugar with your tea?"

"I think there's one of those sweeteners in the yellow packets." Natalie wagged her finger at the credenza.

"Got it." Nicole handed her the cup and the packet of sweetener. "I'm ready for you to visit the evidence-receiving room whenever you like next week."

Natalie picked up a blueberry that had fallen out of her scone from the napkin and popped it in her mouth. Should she tell Nicole now that someone else would be handling the audit? If she did, she'd have to explain why. "I'll let you know."

"I heard Michael's dog, Peaches, came back home." Nicole took a sip of tea, her eyes wide over the rim of the cup. "How crazy is that?"

"So crazy." Natalie picked up the last chunk of scone on her napkin and finished it off. Then she dabbed the crumbs with her fingertips and sucked them from her fingers. "The sheriff's department is going to check out the dog, but there won't be any evidence after this much time."

"I heard the dog actually came back with Raine's bracelet on her collar. I'm sure RJ will be happy to get that back." Nicole took another drink of her tea, holding up her pinkie finger.

Natalie shook her head. How did Nicole know this? "Wait, what? Raine's boyfriend? What bracelet?"

The room felt hot all of a sudden, and Natalie pressed a hand against her forehead, surprised to feel it dampened with sweat.

"Yeah, RJ. Raine's boyfriend. He'd given her a diamond tennis bracelet as a gift—probably stolen. RJ was a criminal, and Raine was no better. She was a bad person, Natalie. I don't know why Michael feels so guilty about her death." Nicole shrugged. "Anyway, RJ said that bracelet was missing when Raine's body was found. Most people thought he was just trying to run some insurance scam, but I guess the dog showed up with the bracelet."

"Who told you that?" Natalie winced as a sharp pain lanced her gut. Peaches had Alma's bracelet on her collar, not a diamond tennis bracelet.

"Michael told me." Nicole dabbed her lips primly. "Michael tells me everything, Natalie. We're quite close."

A wave of nausea passed through Natalie's body, making her shudder. She grabbed onto the edge of the table, knocking over her tea.

"Are you okay?" Nicole scooted back from the tea dripping off the table onto the floor. "You look sick."

"I—I feel…" Natalie cried in agony as another cramp twisted her stomach.

"Don't worry, Natalie. I'm not going to let you die alone like Rachelle."

"Are you going to call an ambulance? I think I need an ambulance."

"Ambulance?"

Natalie unfolded her body and met Nicole's eyes. Dread pounded against her temples. Where had she seen that evil dark glare before?

Nicole stood and grabbed Natalie's arm. "I'm not going to call an ambulance, but I am going to take you someplace I'm sure you've been dreaming of for a long time, Nat."

MICHAEL RUSHED FROM Shady View to his car, tapping Natalie's number on his phone. They had some real evidence, along with Natalie's information about the pendant. Rachelle must've seen Nicole here and wondered why she'd never told anyone about having a father in town. As far as he could remember, Nicole never mentioned family and barely mentioned her dead husband.

Natalie's phone rang and flipped over to voice mail. Was she still angry at him? Did she really believe he'd ratted her out?

He tossed his phone into his cupholder, where it promptly rang. He grabbed it without checking. "Natalie?"

"Sorry to disappoint. It's your sister. Where have you been? I've been calling you for about fifteen minutes."

"Is Ivy okay?"

"Ivy's fine. I just wanted to let you know that someone picked up Peaches."

Michael's heart went back to normal beats per minute once Molly had verified Ivy was fine. She really needed to learn to start the conversation that way. "Okay, fine. I didn't realize they'd be taking her. I thought they'd look at her at the house. I mean, what are they going to do to her?"

"Not sure, but I don't trust them."

"Why not?" Michael started the car. He had to get to Natalie's hotel room to tell her about

Nicole before she left. An aching gulf opened in Michael's chest at the thought of Natalie already on her way back to DC.

"Because the lady who took Peaches was weird."

"Coming from you, I can't imagine."

"Well, she brought scones. Who brings baked goods to pick up an animal for forensic examination. Was she afraid we'd say no, or something?"

Michael slammed on his brakes. "She brought scones?"

"That's what I said, and she really wanted us to try some before she took the dog. I mean, that's weird, right?"

Michael wiped his mouth with the back of his hand. "Did you eat any? Did Ivy?"

"You must think I'm an idiot. Of course not."

"D-did this woman show you a badge?"

"See, there you go again." Molly huffed out a breath. "She had a badge like yours from the Washington State Patrol. You ever bring anyone scones?"

Michael's stomach dropped to his knees. "Dark brown, curly hair? Tall?"

"Yeah, you know her? Nicole something. Sorry, I didn't catch the last name."

Stabbing two fingers against his temple, Michael asked, "She took Peaches? Is that all? Did she get near Ivy?"

"What do you mean?"

Michael spluttered, "Did that woman get anywhere near my daughter?"

Molly gasped. "No. What's going on Michael? Should I call the police?"

"For what? Kidnapping a dog? Just lock the doors, Molly, and don't let Ivy out of your sight. Have you heard from Natalie at all today? Did she come by the house?"

"I don't like this, Michael. Should I throw away the scones?"

"She left them there? Dump them in a plastic bag and put them out of Ivy's reach. Don't throw them away."

Michael's mind raced on the way to Natalie's hotel. He'd been hoping she hadn't left for DC yet, but now he was hoping she had. Why had Nicole come to his place with those scones? Had she shown up to harm Molly and Ivy? Had she always been planning to take Peaches, or was that plan B when Molly wouldn't touch the scones?

A half hour later, wheeled into the hotel parking lot and surveyed it for Natalie's rental car. He didn't see it, but that didn't mean she'd left. The hotel had a parking structure, and she may have parked there with this rain coming on…or to load up her suitcases more easily.

He marched into the lobby and hung back as the reception clerk handled a customer. When she was free, Michael approached the counter. "I'm wondering if you can tell me whether a guest checked out today?"

The woman pulled her keyboard toward her. "Name?"

"Natalie Brunetti."

"Ooh." The clerk glanced up, her bottom lip between her teeth. "Ms. Brunetti is still a guest, but she wasn't feeling well."

Michael swallowed. "She's had a few…incidents since coming to town. Is she in her room? I have the number. I'll go up."

As he started to turn away, the clerk stopped him. "She's not here. Her friend took her to urgent care."

Michael felt the blood drain from his face. "Her friend?"

"Yes, so sweet. I just caught them going out the side door. The friend had her arm around Ms. Brunetti and was helping her walk, half carrying her."

For the second time that day, Michael scrolled through his photos. "What was wrong with her? Was she injured?"

"No, she was ill—stomach flu, I think." The woman's face paled when she met Michael's gaze. "I—I offered to call an ambulance, but her friend seemed to have a handle on the situation."

"This friend?" Michael thrust his phone in front of the hotel clerk's face.

"I think so. She had a hood pulled over her head. I told her about the urgent care down the street, so close. You should be able to find them there."

"Thank you." Michael staggered through the lobby. They wouldn't be at the urgent care. What did Nicole plan to do with Natalie? If she just wanted to kill her, why not poison her and leave her in the hotel room? She didn't want anyone to find Natalie before the poison killed her.

He pressed a fist to his mouth. Think. Where would Nicole take her? The most likely place would be Devil's Edge Trail. That's where she'd lured her before, or at least to the parking lot.

This time he needed a weapon to confront her, especially if Natalie was in a debilitated state. He got on the phone to his sister. "Molly, you still have that gun you brought with you?"

"Why do you need a gun?"

"I think, no, I know, Nicole took Natalie."

"What?" Molly squeaked. "The crazy scone lady? Should I call the police?"

"Yeah, yeah. I'm on my way back. Get that gun loaded and ready for me. Tell the sheriff's patrol that you're concerned about Nicole Meloan and you'd like a wellness check. They'll know her address. At least they can look there while I try the woods."

"I'm on it, Michael."

Ten minutes later, Michael screamed to a stop in front of his house. Before he could even get out of the car, Molly was running down the steps with her gun in her hand.

"I got it from the safe, along with the ammo. I didn't want to load it in the house with Ivy there." She held the gun out to him, barrel down, and pressed a box of ammo into his hand. "Why would Nicole be taking Natalie to the woods? What's going on?"

"I'll tell you about it later. I need to start looking for them."

"You're going to search the whole forest around here? How's that going to work out?"

"I don't have a choice." Michael grabbed his hair as the task at hand overwhelmed him. He'd start in the parking lot, near the playground equipment, and then hike down the trail. It's the only place that made sense. But Nicole didn't make sense. None of it did.

"Michael, Michael." Molly dragged on his arm. "Does Nicole still have Peaches?"

"I have no clue. I'm a little more concerned about Natalie."

Her grip on him tightened. "If that witch still

has Peaches, you can find out exactly where she is."

"Peaches is no bloodhound, Molly. She's a pug."

"I bought Peaches a new collar this morning, and I put a GPS tracking tag on her." She tapped on her phone's screen and waved the device in his face. "She's on the move, Michael."

He took the phone from his sister, grabbed her face with his hands and kissed her on the forehead. "You're a genius."

THE CAR JOSTLED along the unpaved road, and Natalie clutched her stomach. The sharp pains seemed to be receding, but every few minutes her gut would cramp, and she'd let out a low moan.

Peaches had climbed from the back seat to the front and huddled in Natalie's lap. Did the dog remember her from the other day? Why did Nicole have Peaches? Where were they going?

The car stopped so abruptly, Natalie lurched forward, pulling against her shoulder strap. She grabbed the little dog to keep her from sliding to the floor.

If she had the strength, she'd take Peaches, escape from the car and start running. But she had very little strength. Whatever Nicole had slipped into those scones had done a number on her stomach. Arsenic, she'd guess. If she hadn't ingested enough to kill her, the symptoms should dissipate. She'd already vomited twice, which helped clear the poison from her body.

Before she had any more time to contemplate her predicament, Nicole yanked open the passenger side, leaned across her and unhitched her seat belt. "Get out."

Natalie held on to Peaches, tucking her beneath one arm, as she lurched out of the car.

Nicole shoved her, and she tripped, almost falling. Peaches squirmed out of her arms but didn't run away.

"Start walking, Nat." Nicole flashed a knife as she gestured to the path.

Natalie knew this path. It led to the abandoned sawmill. The county had thrown a chain-link fence around it, but people over the years had cut through and trampled the fence so that she and Nicole walked across it now.

The dilapidated chip loader and tower stood like old companions, sentries outlined against the gray sky as the sun began to sink. A chill permeated her skin, giving rise to goose bumps, and she sank to her knees and retched. She didn't want to be here.

"Let's go, Natalie. I think you must've been searching for this place for a long time."

Shaking her head, Natalie wiped the hand

across her mouth. "What is John Westfall to you?"

"He's my father. I had to do whatever I could to protect my father…up to a point."

"So…you what? Destroyed evidence of his crimes? He was a serial killer. He murdered three young women. How could you protect someone like that?"

"Four, but who's counting, really? Not the King County Sheriff's Department." She brandished the knife. "Keep walking toward the chip tower."

Natalie swayed to her feet and judged the distance between her and the knife, aimed at her chest. "How did you find out?"

"About my father? After the very first killing, which was before Katie's. She was a sex worker, though. Nobody cared much about her. He should've stuck with those. I kept protecting him while I worked as an intern at the forensics lab, but he kept getting sloppier and sloppier. Thought he was so clever with the jewelry. I knew those would connect his victims, so I made them disappear."

"Why did he stop? It must've happened about the time he had his accident." Natalie's trembling legs couldn't carry her much farther, so she plopped down on a rotting log, which creaked beneath her.

"Accident." Nicole let out a nasty laugh. "That was no accident. I pushed him out of the boat. Unfortunately, there was a boat nearby, and some guy saved him…sort of. Well, you saw him. Worthless now."

Bile filled Natalie's mouth, and she spit to the side. "You tried to kill your own father to stop him from murdering people. Why not just turn him in?"

"And pay for lawyers, and have my reputation ruined?" Nicole glanced down. "Where'd that dog go?"

"What happened to your husband, Nicole?" Natalie clenched her teeth. She might as well find out everything now, and Nicole might as well tell her.

"He killed himself with a little help from me. He'd discovered my secrets. He was going to turn me in. Can you believe that?"

"You tried to kill your father and killed your husband to protect yourself." Natalie heard a rustle in the bushes and caught the gleam of Peaches's eyes. She also saw the toe of a boot. She dragged her gaze away quickly. Was there someone out there? She just hoped it wasn't someone helping Nicole.

"No, I was trying to protect my father. I'm always doing things for other people."

"Michael's wife?"

"Protecting Michael." Nicole raised her chin, her nostrils flaring. "She was a slut who didn't deserve him. She was making his life hell with the custody battle over Ivy. I just thought the jewelry would be a nice tribute to dear old dad. He still had that piece-of-junk bracelet he'd taken from that last girl."

Natalie caught her breath. "You're in love with Michael."

"And he's in love with me." She swung the knife at Natalie. "You coming in here trying to destroy his lab, his reputation. I'm not going to allow that."

Natalie laughed until a sharp pain in her side made her gasp. "There you go again. You're not killing me to protect Michael. It's all for yourself. Just like you killed Rachelle, so she wouldn't tell anyone that you were visiting Shady View. Is that the only reason? Had Rachelle discovered something about you at the lab?"

"Shut up, Natalie. I'm tired of this."

As Nicole turned her attention to the wood-chip tower, Natalie glanced toward the opening where she'd seen the boots. If Nicole had someone waiting in the wings to help her, he hadn't made his presence known yet. And if she did have an assistant in the woods, why didn't Peaches bark at him?

Her heart leaped with a shot of optimism but

soon sunk. Who would be out here? Who would know where she was? Michael didn't even know about the connection between Nicole and John Westfall. Maybe if she hadn't lashed out at him, they could've stayed together and worked things through—everything.

Nicole narrowed her eyes at her. "Are you feeling well enough to climb to the top of the tower?"

"I'm not climbing up there." Natalie laughed. "If you want to dump my dead body in that wood-chip tower, you're going to have to lug me up there yourself. Good luck with that.

"I would've thought you'd want to go up there after all this time."

"What are you…?" Natalie swallowed as her gaze shifted to the rickety structure. "Wh-why would I want to go there?"

"C'mon, Natalie. You've done such a good job of figuring out everything else. You can't put the last piece of the puzzle in place? You don't see the poetic justice of coming back here to find your missing friend only to join her?"

Natalie dragged herself to her feet, the adrenaline of anger and fear replacing the poison in her body, making her strong. "No!"

"Yes." Nicole held the knife aloft.

Natalie sobbed, tears streaming down her

face, her throat thick with them. "No, no, no. Katie's not in there."

Nicole clicked her tongue. "She's been in there for fourteen years while you left and went on with your life."

A scream tore from Natalie's throat as she hurled herself at Nicole, at the blade pointing straight at her broken heart. Before she could tackle Nicole, before the blade made contact with her skin, a loud pop came from behind her, the sound deafening.

Nicole crumpled in front of her, a surprised look on her face, blood pumping from the carotid artery in her neck.

Natalie flattened her body on the ground and twisted her head around as Peaches waddled toward her and licked the tears from her cheek. Pulling Peaches against her chest, Natalie rolled onto her back.

Michael emerged from the tree line, a gun in his hand, now pointing at the prone figure of Nicole on the ground, the blood from her throat no longer pumping.

"She's dead." Natalie clambered to her knees, and Michael dropped beside her, taking her in his arms.

"Scared the hell out of me when you charged her." He buried his face in her curls.

"How did you know where to find us?"

He reached down to Peaches and flicked her collar. "Molly put a GPS tag on her this morning. I was praying all the way here that she hadn't just dumped the dog somewhere."

"Michael." Natalie sniffed as she pointed to the stark, ugly chip tower. "Katie's in there."

He stroked her back. "I know, my love. You found her."

Epilogue

Stretching her toes toward the fire burning in Michael's fireplace, Natalie scratched Peaches under the chin. "You've had too much excitement, pup. You deserve to relax and get belly rubs."

"She looks like she's put on a few pounds, right?" Molly came from the kitchen, carrying a tray with three mugs of hot cocoa and a sippy cup.

"Peaches looks great. Thanks for looking after her, Molly. I know you're more of a cat person." Michael took the sippy cup from the tray and held it for Ivy, snuggled against his side.

"And thanks for getting her that GPS tag. Michael never would've found me without it."

Molly had scattered mini marshmallows on the tray for Ivy, whose cup had a lid on it. Ivy picked one up and shoved it into her mouth.

Natalie smiled as she took a sip of her own cocoa. "Is that good, Ivy?"

Ivy's head dipped shyly to her chest, and she

looked up at Natalie through her eyelashes. "Mmm."

Then she seemed to make a decision. Ivy collected a handful of the little marshmallows and slid off the couch. She toddled up to Natalie and crouched beside her. "S'mellows?"

"I'd love some marshmallows." Natalie held out her hand, and Ivy dumped several sticky, smooshed marshmallows into her palm before running back to Michael and burying her head in his lap.

Michael grinned at Natalie. "You don't have to eat those."

"Are you kidding? This is when they're the best." She threw the marshmallows into her mouth and chewed, smacking loudly until Ivy turned her head and peeked at her.

Natalie felt a warm wave wash through her body that had nothing to do with the fire crackling in the grate. For the past few weeks, Ivy had looked at her with some interest but had kept her distance...until now. This progress with Michael's daughter shored up Natalie's belief that she'd made the right decision to give up her job with the FBI and move back to Marysville.

Molly cupped her own mug with both hands. "I still don't understand why Nicole came over here and took Peaches."

"I think Peaches gave her an excuse to show

up here and make some kind of assessment." Michael twirled a lock of Ivy's hair around his finger. "If she could've convinced you and Ivy to eat those scones, she may have thought that would've given her some leverage over me or at least distracted me from digging any further into John Westfall. When that didn't happen, she sort of had to take Peaches with her."

"I'm glad she did." Natalie stroked the dog's ears. "Wish I had been able to say no to the scones. Do you think she also poisoned those cookies? Is that why Rachelle went home sick that day?"

Michael shrugged. "Possibly, but nobody else got sick at the office."

"She could've selected some cookies specifically for Rachelle. Did she—" Molly glanced at Ivy, who seemed alert, her gaze tracking back and forth between each speaker "—use the old scone trick on Rachelle?"

"Soup." Natalie took a sip of cocoa and shivered.

Pointing to Ivy, Molly said, "It's bedtime for my favorite niece."

"I'll get her ready." Michael stood, lifting Ivy in his arms.

"I'll give her a bath." Molly put her mug on the mantel. "You two should have some alone time before Natalie goes back to DC."

Michael handed off Ivy to his sister, giving her a one-armed hug in the process. "You're the best, Molly."

"Hold that thought." Molly held up one finger. "I may be asking for a loan shortly."

Natalie stood also, and kissed Ivy on her soft cheek. "Good night, Ivy."

Ivy waved by opening and closing her hand, as Molly carried her to the back of the house.

Michael patted the cushion next to him. "Molly's right. You're leaving tomorrow, and I feel like I've barely had any time with you—hospital visits, police interviews, TV interviews, meetings with the FBI."

She curled up next to him and rested her head on his shoulder. "It's been a hectic few weeks."

"Have you recovered from your meeting with Katie's parents?"

Natalie stared into the fire. Mr. and Mrs. Fellows had come out to Washington to claim their daughter's remains and had requested a meeting with her. She didn't know what to expect, but they couldn't have been more kind. They didn't hate her. They never blamed her for Katie's disappearance, and they were so grateful that Natalie had never given up on their daughter.

Natalie hadn't suffered from one nightmare since that meeting.

"Talking with them was special. Maybe finding out where Katie's body had been all this time made me feel better, but seeing their relief was a hundred times more important. It should've always been about them, not me."

"But you felt the guilt." He kissed the top of her head. "It was about you."

"And you?" She turned her head and placed a finger on his lips. "You didn't replace one set of guilty feelings with another, did you? You never gave Nicole any encouragement. You had no way of knowing she'd fixated on you."

"I don't feel guilty. Some things are just out of our control." He kissed her fingertips, and then bent his head to kiss her mouth. "That's why when fate does put something, or someone, in your path, you grab it with both hands and never let it go."

"I feel the same way." She cupped his chin with one hand. "Terrible circumstances drew us together, forged something between us that can't break. Fate."

A small hand on Natalie's knee ended her kiss with Michael, and she turned to find Ivy standing next to the couch, fresh bath scent floating from her baby-soft hair.

Molly rushed from the back. "Sorry. Had my back turned, picking out books, and she took off."

Ivy pointed at Natalie. "Nat read."

Sitting forward, Michael asked, "Do you want Nat to read you a bedtime story, Ivy?"

Ivy nodded as she curled her fingers around Natalie's hand.

Natalie brushed Michael's cheek. "Can fate wait another fifteen minutes?"

"What's fifteen minutes when you've promised me a lifetime?"

Natalie stood, hitching Ivy on her hip. She blew Michael a kiss as she waltzed his little girl off to bed. It seemed only right that she'd returned to the place that had stolen her happiness only to replace that emptiness with a new life, overflowing with joy. Fate. Timing. Serendipity. Whatever.

She'd take it.

* * * * *